Maya (sitting on the edge of her bed, her arms wrapped around her aching body, whispering to herself): "I don't feel strong."

Her Reflection (watching her from the mirror, tilting its head): "Why? Just Because you're afraid?"

Maya (nodding, voice barely above a whisper): "Yes. I'm terrified. Of this pain. Of what's coming next. Of never getting better."

Her Reflection (gently): "And you think being afraid makes you weak?"

Maya (frustrated, gripping the bedsheet in her fists): "Isn't that what weakness is? Breaking down? Feeling helpless?"

Her Reflection (shaking its head): "No. Weak is refusing to face what's in front of you. Weak is giving up before you even try. But you? You've been facing this every single day."

Maya (scoffing, looking away): "Facing it? I cry, I panic, I question everything. That's not strength."

Her Reflection (stepping closer, voice firm): "Yes, it is. Strong isn't the person who isn't afraid of anything. That's a lie we tell ourselves. Strong is the person who *is afraid but keeps going anyway. Strong is knowing the battle is hard but if I can't make it out of this?"*

Her Reflection (softly, reassuringly): *"You can. And deep down, you know you will."*

Maya (whispering, as if testing the words out loud): *"I will."*

Her Reflection (smiling faintly): *"That's strength."*

Maya exhaled, letting the words settle inside her. Maybe she didn't have all the answers. But she was still here. Still fighting. And maybe, just maybe, that was enough.

Dedicated to the ones who believed in me even
when I myself couldn't.

Your faith made this possible.

Table of Contents

Acknowledgements

I would like to express my heartfelt gratitude to the people who have been instrumental in the completion of this book (and have made my life easier and more meaningful)

First and foremost, my sincere thanks to **Swara Shah**, who took the time to read the entire manuscript before publication. Your thoughtful feedback helped shape the final version of this book. There were moments when I felt unsure about the path I was taking with this project, but your insightful suggestions were like a compass, always pointing me in the right direction. In many ways, I consider you my younger sister—your wisdom, care, and belief in me have made all the difference.

I am deeply grateful to **Sanskruti Patel** for standing by me in every important decision I've made in life. Your unwavering support has been a source of strength, especially when I doubted myself. You've been the lighthouse in the storm, guiding me toward clarity even in the most confusing moments. There are some people in life who become more than just friends—they become family, and you are certainly one of those rare people to me.

A special thank you to **Parth Mehta** for your constant encouragement and belief in me. There were days when the thought of writing this book felt overwhelming, but your faith in me inspired me to keep going. You were the voice in my head telling me, "You've got this," even when I wasn't sure I did.

To **Bhargavi Mevada**, thank you for always being there when I needed someone the most. Your presence has been like a warm blanket on cold nights. I can't tell you how many times your friendship has been the anchor that kept me grounded. Your kindness and patience never went unnoticed.In many ways, I consider you not just a friend, but an elder sister.

My heartfelt thanks to **Parth Patel**, whose guidance has been like the steady rhythm of a song I always want to dance to. Through life's ups and downs, your words of encouragement have reminded me that I am never truly alone in this journey. You've been a constant source of wisdom and reassurance, and for that, I am forever grateful.

I want to express my sincere appreciation to **Bhavya Kamdar** for proving that a friend in need is a friend indeed, always standing by me in times of need.

To **Paresh Wadhvani**, **Yesha Parmar**, and **Harshil Panchal**, your presence has been a constant source of comfort during some of my toughest times. Your unwavering support and humor have been like a breath of fresh air, lifting me up when I needed it most and making even the darkest days feel a little brighter.

To **Meera ma'am** and **Sonal didi**, you may have been a part of my life for only a short period, but the impact you've had on me is immeasurable.I am truly grateful for the wisdom you shared and the strength you helped me find in myself, even in such a brief time.

Cannot thank enough to **Kalgi Trivedi** & **Nisarg Khatri**, whose love and encouragement have been a constant source of strength. Your belief in me, your support in both the small and big moments, has been invaluable. You've shown me what it means to be truly present for someone, offering both wisdom and laughter when I needed it the most. I'm so grateful to have you both in my life.

Lastly, words like 'thank you' feel far too small to express the depth of my gratitude for everything **my parents** have done for me. Their love, support, and unwavering belief in me have been the bedrock upon which all my achievements stand. Their strength, wisdom, and selflessness have been the roots that keep me grounded, no matter where life takes me. I am truly blessed beyond measure to have them by my side, guiding me with their infinite care.

I feel truly fortunate to be surrounded by such **amazing people in my life**, whose love and care have been a constant source of strength.

PREFACE

This book was born out of a desire to inspire and remind readers of their own potential. At its heart, it carries a simple but powerful message: *If Maya can, then you can too*.

Maya's journey is one of courage, bravery and optimism in the face of illness. She faced moments that tested her strength, both physically and emotionally. Through every trial, she discovered that even the darkest night will end and the sun will rise. This book is a testament to the inner strength we all possess, even when we tend to be our most fragile and vulnerable self.

My hope is that Maya's story will serve as a reminder that no matter how overwhelming fear or pain may seem, it can be conquered. We can rise above all the odds - our struggles, face our fears, and come out stronger on the other side.

This is not just Maya's story—it's a story for anyone who has ever faced adversity and wondered if they could make it through. And it's here to tell you: **yes, you can.**

If Maya's journey can inspire even one reader to believe in their own ability to endure and thrive, then this book has accomplished its purpose.

INTRODUCTION

Maya is a young woman much like any other—full of dreams, aspirations, and a deep appreciation for the simple joys of life. She cherished the moments spent with her family, shared laughter with close friends, and found peace in the routine of her everyday existence. Life, for her, was a blend of hope, love, and gratitude. However, one day, everything changed and her world went upside down - the day when she was detected with an unexpected diagnosis.

What began as small, dismissible symptoms spiraled into a life defined by hospital visits, complex treatments, and the daunting uncertainty of a long-term illness. The familiar, comfortable rhythm of her life gave way to a relentless battle against her own body. Yet, in the midst of this turmoil, Maya held onto something even more powerful—**her faith.** It became her anchor as she faced one challenge after another, giving her strength whenever her body faltered. Alongside this faith, Maya discovered a deeper sense of gratitude—not just for the good days, but for every small victory, every moment of relief, and the unwavering support of those around her.

This is the story of how her resilience, gratitude, and faith carried her through the darkest times, enabling her to navigate the hardships of illness while holding on to the hope of reclaiming her life.

Chapter 1 Your Scars - Your Strength

In hidden places, strength takes flight,

Scars tell stories of our fight.

Through pain we rise, our spirits grow,

Changed but stronger, we face the flow.

Maya - a middle class girl was a source of joy to those around her, yet her own life was shaped by silent battles that tested her spirit from an early age. She had been dealt a difficult hand, living with a stubborn skin condition that clung to her like a shadow for a decade. While other children ran freely under the sun, chasing dreams without a care, Maya spent her days navigating hospital corridors, trading playdates for treatments.

Her fate led her down a road only few had to take, one paved with patience and endurance. While she learned to carry her burdens with quiet strength, the world around her was not always kind. People—some unknowingly, others without hesitation—made remarks that stung like nettles. The whispers followed her family wherever they went, laced with questions that revealed the unkind weight of society's expectations.

And so, in hushed gatherings and casual conversations, her parents found themselves answering questions that cut deeper than the condition itself—questions that reduced their daughter to nothing more than her illness.

(Maya's parents are sitting with some relatives and neighbors. Maya, now about ten years old, is playing nearby, pretending not to listen. But every word seeps into her little heart like ink on paper.)

Aunt Reema (whispering, but loud enough to be heard): *"I feel so bad for you both. Such a sweet girl, but… you must be worried."*

Maya's mother (forcing a smile): *"Worried? About what?"*

Aunt Reema: *"You know… her condition. It's one thing now, but later? When it's time for marriage? People can be cruel."*

Neighbor, shaking their head: *"Exactly. Society doesn't accept such things easily. How will you find a boy for her?"*

Maya's father (stiffly): *"She's ten. Maybe we should worry about her dreams before worrying about her wedding."*

Uncle Rakesh (scoffing): *"That's easy for you to say. But let's be real, no matter how educated or independent a girl is, marriage is still important. Who will accept her with a skin disease like that?"*

Maya's mother (her voice now firm): *"Whoever can see beyond the surface. And if no one does, then so be it—she'll still shine on her own."*

Aunt Reema (sighing, shaking her head): *"You're being too modern. A mother has to be practical."*

Maya's father (leaning forward, voice steady):
"Practical? Practical would be teaching her that she is more than her skin. Practical would be making sure she knows she is whole, standing on her own legs, courageous enough to face the world's cruelty, whenever it hits her. "

Neighbor (glancing at Maya, who is still pretending not to listen): *"Poor thing. I just hope she doesn't start believing she's different."*

Maya (finally looking up, her voice clear and unwavering): *"But I am different. And that's not a bad thing."*

(A brief silence follows. The adults exchange glances. Her parents smile—because in that moment, they know that no matter what the world says, Maya has already learned to stand tall.)

Despite the hardships, she stood tall, believing in her own beauty and worth. She knew that beauty was more than just skin-deep and refused to let anyone define her worth. With wisdom far beyond her years, she came to understand that grace, resilience, and strength are often born from life's toughest trials. From blooming in the midst of her challenges, to rising like a lotus rising through muddy waters, radiating confidence and poise even when the world around her seemed determined to knock her down, Maya already won at life.

For much of her childhood, it seemed as if no treatment could bring her the relief she so desperately sought. Over the span of ten long years, she consulted with nine different specialists, each offering new hope with every visit, but that hope was always quickly dashed. It became a decade marked by frustrations and false starts, as each new doctor proposed treatments and solutions that ultimately fell short.

Despite these constant disappointments, Maya refused to let the setbacks break her spirit. Where many would have crumbled under the weight of so many failures, she chose to learn and grow instead. Every misstep, every failed treatment, became a lesson—a hard-earned truth that shaped her into someone who could face even greater challenges with an unshakable resolve.

"I have not failed. I've just found 10,000 ways that won't work."

Thomas Edison

Rather than succumbing to the discouragement that could have easily overtaken her, Maya developed a remarkable capacity to adapt,adapt the way of living she never thought of facing, adapt the situation she never thought she would be put in. Each time a treatment failed, she didn't see it as an end but as a new beginning. She learned to re-evaluate each situation, to analyze what had gone wrong, and to approach her challenges from a different, more determined perspective. Over time, what others might have seen as failures, Maya saw as stepping stones in her personal growth. These experiences tested her patience and perseverance but at the same time, gave her an invaluable understanding of resilience. She discovered that progress, no matter how slow or elusive it seemed, was still progress—and that each obstacle could be overcome with persistence, adaptability, if only one has the right mindset.

"You may encounter many defeats, but you must not be defeated. In fact, it may be necessary to encounter the defeats, so you can know who you are, what you can rise from, how you can still come out of it."

Maya Angelou

As Maya emerged from one battle stronger than ever, she believed she had weathered life's worst storms. But the horizon held darker clouds, challenges that would test her in ways she couldn't yet fathom. What lay ahead? Could the lessons of her past prepare her for the trials still to come?

Chapter 2 Twist of Fate

Dreams of normalcy,

Shattered by a cold diagnosis,

Unknown paths await.

Every Sunday morning felt like a celebration in her presence. Maya had a way of making even the simplest gatherings feel special, filling the air with her infectious energy and contagious laugh. She loved spending time with her family, whether it was sitting together in the living room, reminiscing about old memories, or planning the week ahead with a mix of practicality and humour. Her stories, filled with wit and warmth, always left everyone laughing.

Maya had always been an epitome of happiness and the centre of attraction at all the places she visited, for all the people she met and filled the air with the smell of her ever growing kindness for others. Her laughter was contagious, filling the room with her irresistible energy. On most evenings, she would gather her closest friends around a cozy terrace, where the aroma of freshly brewed chai filled the air. They would sit in a warm circle, sharing stories of childhood mischiefs and festive celebrations-some real, some hilariously exaggerated-while the night breeze played with their hair. She had a way of making even the simplest moments feel like a grand celebration, as if life itself was a series of small joys strung together by her boundless enthusiasm.

Her unique ability to bring people together, making them feel valued and understood, ensuring that every person in the room felt they were exactly where they were meant to be. Her presence would turn an ordinary

Sunday into something memorable, a time everyone looked forward to simply because of her presence.

Her gatherings were more than just celebrations-they were a reflection of her care and love. She always ensured that her friends and family were well taken care of, from making sure everyone had their favourite snacks to checking in on them with a gentle word or a thoughtful gesture. Her energy was contagious, turning every occasion worth cherishing, where everyone felt like they were part of something truly special, because she made sure they knew they were.

Maya sat at her desk, the pen trembling in her hand as she tried to jot down the words that refused to flow out of it. Her illness had stolen so much from her—her carefree days, her confidence, even her ability to write without pain—but it hadn't taken her resolve.

This was her story, a story she would tell, no matter how long it took. Maya was like any other young woman, filled with hopes, dreams, and the desire to live a normal life. She loved spending time with her family, had a close group of friends, and enjoyed the simple pleasures that life offered. But everything changed when the doctors delivered the news of her illness. Suddenly, the normalcy she once cherished was replaced by hospital visits, medical treatments, and a looming fear of the unknown.

At first, Maya found herself consumed by fear and confusion, the idea of living with a chronic illness seemed unimaginable. The future she had envisioned now felt distant and uncertain. Each day brought new challenges-some physical, like the pain and fatigue from treatments, and others emotional, like the anxiety that crept into her thoughts late at night. Her once vibrant spirit began to dull as she struggled to come to terms with her condition.

"Faith is taking the first step even when you don't see the whole staircase."

Martin Luther King Jr.

This is not just a story of illness -it's a story of strength. Despite the overwhelming fear and uncertainty, Maya refused to let her diagnosis define her.

She was the kind of person who could see through the masks people wore, understanding the pain or confusion they were trying to hide. When her friends felt lost, she didn't just offer generic advice; she took the time to listen deeply, to really understand their situation before speaking. Her words were always thoughtful, tailored to what each person needed to hear, and delivered with a sincerity that made her advice resonate on a deeper level. It wasn't just about solving problems; it was about making her friends feel seen and understood, reminding them that they weren't alone in their struggles. Her guidance was like a steady hand on the shoulder, reassuring them that no matter how difficult things seemed, they could find their way through.

What made her so remarkable was that she did this even when she was struggling herself. She had her own battles-times when she felt overwhelmed, when the weight of her own challenges threatened to pull her under. However, she never let that stop her from being there for others. Even when she needed someone to lean on, she would set aside her own needs to help those she cared about. It was as if her compassion for others gave her the strength to keep going, to push through her own pain so she could lift others out of theirs.

Even when Maya was struggling herself, she found ways to lift others. She remembered one evening when a long lost friend called her, overwhelmed by her own challenges.

(Maya is lying on her bed, her body aching. Her phone buzzes—it's an old friend, Ayesha. They haven't spoken in a while.)

Maya (picking up, forcing a light tone): *"Ayesha! It's been ages. What's up?"*

Ayesha (her voice shaky): *"Maya… I didn't know who else to call."*

Maya (sitting up, concern lacing her voice): *"Hey, hey. What happened?"*

Ayesha (sniffling): *"Everything feels like it's falling apart. I feel like I'm drowning, and no matter what I do,* *nothing gets better. I just… I don't know how much longer I can take this."*

Maya (softly, but firmly): *"Take a deep breath, Ayesha. You don't have to figure everything out right now. Just tell me what's going on."*

Ayesha (exhaling shakily): *"It's everything—work, relationship, my health… I feel like I'm failing at all of it. And no one understands."*

Maya (nodding, though Ayesha can't see her): *"I hear you. And I know how heavy it gets when it feels like you're carrying everything alone."*

Ayesha (quietly): *"But how do you do it, Maya? After everything you've been through… How do you keep going?"*

Maya (smiling slightly, despite the ache in her hands): *"Honestly? Some days, I don't know. But I remind myself that even when it feels impossible, I've made it through every bad day so far. And so have you."*

Ayesha (voice steadier now): *"I wish I had your strength."*

Maya: *"You do, Ayesha. You just don't see it yet. But I do."*

Ayesha (sniffles, then chuckles weakly): *"You always make me feel like I can get through anything."*

Maya (smiling softly): *"Because you can."*

(For the first time in a while that night, Ayesha lets out a deep breath, a little lighter than before. And Maya, despite her own pain, feels a quiet warmth in knowing that even in her struggles, she has the power to ease someone else's.)

"The most beautiful people we have known are those who have known defeat, known suffering, known struggle, known loss, and have found their way out of the depths. These persons have an appreciation, a sensitivity, and an understanding of life that fills them with compassion, gentleness, and a deep loving concern. Beautiful people do not just happen."

Elisabeth Kübler-Ross

Her friends often wondered how she did it-how she could be so strong. But that was just who she was. Her love and loyalty were unwavering, a constant source of light in their lives. She didn't expect anything in return; she simply believed in being there for the people she loved, no matter what. In a world where so many people are quick to look out for themselves, she stood out as someone who truly embodied selflessness, always putting others before herself.

"Carry out a random act of kindness, with no expectation of reward, safe in the knowledge that one day someone might do the same for you."

Princess Diana

"The best way to find yourself is to lose yourself in the service of others."

Mahatma Gandhi

Some people, despite their own struggles, become a source of strength for others. They carry unseen burdens yet never let their pain overshadow the needs of those around them. Instead, their struggles deepen their empathy, making them more attuned to the silent suffering of others. They show us that helping others while healing ourselves is not heroism, but humanity. Their example proves that pain doesn't weaken our ability to love—it can strengthen it, turning wounds into wisdom and compassion.

Their example revealed that sometimes, **the greatest healers are those who are healing themselves**, and that our own wounds can become a source of strength if we allow them to.

"The purpose of human life is to serve, and to show compassion and the will to help others."

Albert Schweitzer

Maya's dreams used to feel limitless. She could picture herself climbing mountains, dancing at festivals, and chasing every adventure life had to offer. But after her diagnosis, even climbing the stairs felt like a battle. The vibrant future she'd once envisioned seemed to dim, leaving her uncertain of what lay ahead.

This Maya was not the Maya she had envisioned when she was younger, not the person she thought she would become. Yet, here she was, uncertain about what the future held, grappling with the challenges life had thrown her way. She was a helpless youth, struggling with pain in her hand while trying to write her book and pain in her bones while attempting to run with friends. She was a Maya who felt lost and overwhelmed—a far cry from the vibrant, ambitious person she once hoped to be. *"Why is this happening to me, is this the consequence of my past karmas? What did I do to deserve this pain?"* she would ask herself, staring blankly at the ceiling in the middle of the night, feeling an emptiness that words couldn't fill.

Chapter 3 Unseen Beginnings

Whispers from within,

Diagnosis steals her breath,

Life shifts in one beat.

When Maya was rushed to the hospital, the situation was dire.Her rapidly declining health was evident from the steady deterioration of her haemoglobin levels. Day by day, her haemoglobin count dropped lower, signalling a severe and potentially life-threatening condition. The doctors closely monitored her, trying various treatments to stabilize her, but nothing could stop the relentless decline.

Each passing day, Maya's haemoglobin levels continued to plummet.On the first day, it dropped to 6 g/dl. By the next, it had fallen further to 5 g/dl. Day three saw another sharp decline to 4.8 g/dl. The medical team scrambled to stabilize her, but nothing seemed to halt the relentless drop. Then, one day, the unthinkable happened—her haemoglobin plummeted to a staggering 3.5 g/dl.

(The doctor pulls up a chair beside Maya's hospital bed, his face lined with concern. Maya, pale and exhausted, watches him with weary eyes, her usual sarcasm still flickering beneath the weight of her condition.)

Doctor (gently): *"Maya, how are you feeling today?"*

Maya (raising her hand to her neck, making a slashing motion): *"Six, five, four-point-eight, three-point-five," she murmured, her voice barely above a whisper. "One day, we'll hit zero, and then I guess I'll finally get some rest."*

(The room falls into a heavy silence. The doctor exhales, watching her closely.)

Doctor (leaning forward, voice firm but kind): *"Not on my watch, Maya."*

Maya (giving a weak smirk): *"You can't stop the countdown, Doc."*

Doctor (softly): *"Maybe not. But I can remind you that numbers don't define you. And neither does this illness."*

Maya (closing her eyes briefly, then opening them): *"Then what does?"*

Doctor (meeting her gaze): *"The way you fight. The way you laugh, even now. The way you make jokes that scare half my staff."*

(Maya looks at him for a long moment. She doesn't answer, but she doesn't make another joke either. And for now, that's enough.)

Yet, in the face of these overwhelming odds, Maya remained remarkably calm (and funny). While the medical team did everything in their power to stabilize her, she placed her trust in something beyond their expertise. She had an unwavering belief in the doctors

treating her, but more than that, she had a deep faith in
God. She believed that her life was in divine hands, and
this spiritual conviction gave her strength even when
her body was at its weakest.

Despite the grim prognosis and the astonishment of the
medical professionals around her, she held on. Her
faith became her anchor, a source of hope that
sustained her through the most perilous moments. As
the doctors continued to fight for her survival, she held
tightly to her faith, trusting that she would pull through.

*"Faith is the strength by which a shattered world shall
emerge into the light."*

Helen Keller

As her condition worsened, an alarming new symptom
emerged - her tongue began to turn blue.

This unusual and frightening sign sent a wave of
concern through the medical team. The doctors were
bewildered, struggling to understand what could be
causing such a dramatic change in her condition. They
knew that a blue tongue could indicate severe oxygen

deprivation or other critical health issues, but despite their best efforts, they couldn't immediately pinpoint the underlying cause.

The situation grew more severe as the doctors searched for answers. They ran multiple tests, consulted specialists, and explored every possible avenue to determine the root of her deteriorating health. Yet, the mystery remained unsolved, and her symptoms only seemed to become more concerning with each passing day.

Then, one day, amidst the growing uncertainty and desperation, one of the doctors had a breakthrough. Recalling the possibility of an autoimmune disorder-a condition in which the body's immune system mistakenly attacks its own tissues- the doctor decided to investigate further.

This line of thinking led to the decision to order ANA (Antinuclear Antibody) tests, which are used to detect autoimmune diseases.

When the results came back, they finally had an answer. The tests revealed that Maya was suffering from an autoimmune disease—a condition where the body's own immune system mistakenly attacks healthy tissues, treating them as foreign invaders. In Maya's case, this relentless internal battle had led to the development of rheumatoid arthritis, a chronic inflammatory disorder that primarily affected her joints but also explained the other perplexing symptoms she had been experiencing. The persistent pain in her bones, the swelling in her hands, the fatigue that never seemed to fade—all of it finally made sense.

(Maya's parents sit on either side of her bed, their faces lined with worry. The recent diagnosis of rheumatoid arthritis hangs heavily in the air. Maya, though physically weak, is still sharp enough to sense the unspoken concerns between her parents.)

Maya (breaking the silence): *"So… what's the verdict? Are we telling the entire extended family, or are we keeping this one under wraps?"*

Her mother (hesitant, exchanging a glance with her father): *"Maya, it's not about hiding it, but… you know how they are. They'll make a scene out of this."*

Maya (raising an eyebrow, her voice laced with dry humor): *"You mean like the last time? When I had a skin disease and suddenly half the family became honorary dermatologists overnight?"*

Her father (sighing, rubbing his temples): *"Yes. They panicked, exaggerated, and acted like your life was over. We don't want to go through that again. And more importantly, you don't need that kind of negativity."*

Her mother (softly, reaching for Maya's hand): "They mean well, beta, but they don't understand. They'll act as if this is the end of the world, as if you'll never have a normal life. And we know that's not true."

Maya (smirking): "Oh, I can already hear it—'Who will marry her now?' 'What kind of life will she have?' 'We should find a healer!' Maybe even a few dramatic gasps for good measure."

Her father (squeezing her hand): "But that's what we know you'll be just fine."

Maya (leaning back against the pillows, exhaling deeply): "Look, I get it. We don't need a family-wide panic attack over this. But honestly, I still think you guys are overreacting."

Her mother (frowning): "Maya, this isn't something small. It's a chronic illness. It's going to take adjustments—medications, lifestyle changes…"

Maya (waving a hand dismissively): "Right, right. I get it. But it's not like I'm dying or anything. I mean, come on.Maybe I just need to exercise more. Or get better sleep. You guys are acting like this is some kind of life sentence.

Her mother (softly): "It's not a life sentence, but it is real, Maya. You have to accept it."

Maya (stubbornly crossing her arms): *"I don't have to accept anything. Doctors make mistakes all the time. Maybe it's just stress. Or the weather. Or something temporary. It'll go away."*

Her father (exchanging a worried look with her mother): *"Maya…"*

Maya (firmly, her voice edged with finality): *"I don't have arthritis. I'm not 60, I'm 20. This is just a bad phase. And like all bad phases, it'll pass."*

(Her parents didn't argue, but the room was heavy with unspoken words. They knew denial when they saw it. And right now, Maya was clinging to it like a lifeline.)

The discovery of the autoimmune disease marked a turning point in Maya's treatment, even if she wasn't ready to accept it. With a clear diagnosis, the doctors adjusted her treatment plan to specifically address the underlying cause of her symptoms. Yet, despite the medical certainty, Maya clung to her denial. She took the prescribed medications, but in her mind, it was all precautionary—a mistake that would soon be corrected.

Chapter 4 The stages of grief

Denial clouds the mind,
Anger burns through fading hope,
Acceptance brings peace.

The Kübler-Ross model outlines five stages of grief—
**denial, anger, bargaining, depression, and
acceptance**. Denial, the first stage, is often the mind's
way of shielding itself from a painful reality. It allows a
person to process the truth at their own pace,
cushioning the initial shock. And that was exactly what
Maya was experiencing.

She had always been strong, or at least that's what she
told herself. She was the kind of person who got sick
easily, and whenever she did, she brushed it off as
nothing more than temporary discomfort. So, when the
occasional stiffness in her fingers started creeping in,
she dismissed it.

*"It's just fatigue. I've been working too much. Nothing
serious."*

The swelling in her hands? Probably too much typing.
The dull ache in her joints? Just another sign of a
stressful week. She reasoned that a little rest, maybe
some over-the-counter painkillers, would make it go
away. Arthritis? Absolutely not. That was for older
people, for those who had spent decades straining their
bodies.

But then winter came.

The cold seeped into her bones like an uninvited guest,
settling there, refusing to leave. One morning, as she
reached for her coffee mug, a sharp pain shot through

her fingers. She winced, almost dropping the cup. Her fingers felt stiff, unmovable, as if they no longer belonged to her. She flexed them slowly, biting her lip against the pain.

Still, she shook her head. *No. This isn't arthritis. It's just the cold. Everyone feels a little stiff in the winter.*

She walked over to the mirror, staring at her own reflection, trying to find reassurance in her own eyes.

Maya (to herself): "I don't have arthritis."

Her reflection: "Then what do you have?"

Maya: "Something temporary. Maybe I slept wrong, or maybe it's just the weather."

Her reflection: "Then why does it hurt so much? Why can't you even move your fingers without wincing?"

Maya (defensive): "It's just… I haven't been taking care of myself properly. I need more vitamins, more water, maybe some exercise."

Her reflection (calm, yet firm): "Maya, you know that's not true."

Maya (angrily shaking her head): "No! I'm fine! It's not that bad. It'll pass."

She turned away from the mirror, rubbing her hands as if that simple action could erase the pain. But deep inside, she knew—this wasn't something that would just go away.

Yet, denial was easier. It was comforting. It allowed her to hold on to the illusion that everything was still within her control.

So, she wrapped herself in that illusion, pretending that nothing was wrong.

At least, for now.

Denial had become Maya's silent companion. It was easier to believe that she was just tired, overworked, or that the cold weather was making her joints stiff. It was easier than admitting the truth—that something deeper, something irreversible, was happening inside her body.

She had always prided herself on being independent, on pushing through discomfort. Weakness was never an option. Illness was something that happened to other people, not to her. So, when her fingers throbbed with pain in the middle of the night, she clenched them into fists and willed herself to sleep. When she struggled to open a jar in the kitchen, she laughed it off, making excuses about weak grip strength. When the stiffness in her knees made it difficult to climb stairs, she convinced herself that she just needed to exercise more.

But her body wasn't listening to these justifications.

Denial had shielded her for as long as it could, but that morning, as Maya got ready for an important day at college, something inside her cracked.

As she reached for her coat, her fingers hesitated. The buttons—small, simple, insignificant on any other day—felt like an impossible challenge. She tried once, twice, but her fingers wouldn't cooperate. The stiffness had settled in overnight, making each movement a struggle. The more she tried, the more the pain intensified, a sharp, burning sensation shooting through her joints.

Her breathing grew heavy. Her frustration boiled beneath the surface, hot and suffocating.

"This is ridiculous."

With gritted teeth, she yanked at the fabric, forcing the button through the hole with a sharp, painful twist of her fingers. The sting was immediate, a cruel reminder of her body's betrayal. She hissed in pain, slamming her fists against the dresser.

Why was this happening to her?

Why was something as simple as buttoning a coat turning into an unbearable task?

Tears of frustration welled in her eyes, but she blinked them away. She didn't want to cry. Crying would mean giving in, accepting that something was wrong. And she wasn't ready for that.

But she was angry.

Angry at her body for failing her. Angry at the pain for creeping in and refusing to leave. Angry at the unfairness of it all.

She had always been in control—of her life, her ambitions, her future. And now? Now she couldn't even do something as basic as buttoning her own coat without feeling like her hands were turning against her.

A sharp exhale left her lips, her hands balling into fists. She wanted to throw something, to scream, to demand why this was happening to her.

"No. I won't let this stop me."

The anger still burned inside her, but she refused to surrender to it. She was going to college today, no matter what. She was strong. Yes, She can do this.

At least, that's what she told herself as she grabbed her bag and stormed out the door.

Chapter 5 The cost of the big decision

A step toward hope's light,

Hospital doors swing open,

The price of strength paid.

This unpredictability added a layer of emotional strain on top of the physical pain, leaving Maya feeling not only helpless but frustrated. She had always been someone who valued her independence, yet now she found herself relying on others for tasks she had once taken for granted. The loss of control over her own body and the overwhelming weakness were difficult to accept. The pain disrupted her routines, but more than that, it chipped away at her sense of self. Each day felt like a test of endurance, a challenge to push through the agony and find a way to carry on with her life despite the limitations imposed by the disease.

This period of her life was marked by an ongoing battle between her desire to stay strong and the harsh reality of her symptoms.

Despite diligently following her prescribed treatment, the joint pain showed no signs of easing. In fact, it worsened over time, leaving her feeling increasingly desperate for a solution. The relentless pain in her joints became an overwhelming force in her life, seeping into every aspect of her daily routine. Simple actions like brushing her hair or typing on her computer became excruciating, making her feel as though she was losing control over her body and her independence.

The frustration of seeing no improvement, even after months of treatment, began to weigh heavily on her, both physically and emotionally. She found herself constantly searching for a way out of the pain, longing for relief.

And then, the bargaining began.

"Maybe if I change my diet, the pain will stop." She started eliminating certain foods, hoping that something, *anything*, would make a difference.

"Maybe if I pray more, if I make a deal with the universe, things will get better." She whispered silent promises into the darkness before falling asleep at night. *"If I can just have one pain-free day, I'll do better. I'll be more grateful. I'll be more careful with my body."*

"Maybe the doctors are missing something. Maybe I need a second opinion, a different kind of treatment. Something else has to work."

One day, during a heart-to-heart conversation with a close friend, Maya finally opened up about the depth of her struggles. She shared how exhausting and debilitating the pain had become, how it was affecting her overall quality of life.

Her friend, deeply concerned, listened carefully before suggesting something different—a path she hadn't yet considered. They spoke about Ayurveda, a holistic approach to healing that focused on balancing the body, mind, and spirit. They mentioned that Ayurveda had helped many people manage chronic conditions, particularly those involving pain and inflammation, with treatments tailored to the individual's unique constitution.

Maya latched onto the idea like a lifeline.

"Maybe this is the answer. Maybe this is what I've been missing."

And so, with a fragile kind of hope, she decided to give it a try.

Intrigued by the possibility of finding a new avenue of healing, Maya began to research Ayurveda in earnest. She was drawn to its natural, whole-body approach, which seemed so different from the allopathic treatments she had been undergoing. After careful thought and consultation with Ayurvedic practitioners, Maya made a bold decision: she would discontinue her current allopathic treatment and fully commit to Ayurveda. It was a difficult choice, one that came with its own set of uncertainties, but she had to choose what was right over what was easy. Her intuition told her that this ancient system of medicine might be the key to unlocking the relief she so desperately needed, especially since her current treatment hadn't brought the results she had hoped for.

As she began her Ayurvedic treatment, Maya followed a personalized regimen that included dietary changes, herbal supplements, and practices like yoga and meditation designed to reduce inflammation and promote healing. Initially, she didn't notice much of a difference, but over time, the improvements became undeniable. The joint pain that had once been an unbearable, constant companion started to recede. It didn't vanish overnight, but slowly, day by day, she began to feel lighter, as if a weight had been lifted from her body. Tasks that had seemed impossible, like holding a pen or typing on a keyboard, became manageable once again, she started to see a ray of hope amidst the undeniable chaos once again.

With each passing week, Maya could feel her strength returning. The treatment seemed to be working in ways she had almost given up hoping for. Her body responded to the Ayurvedic practices, and for the first time in a long time, she felt a glimmer of optimism. The unbearable joint pain no longer dictated her every move, and she found herself able to engage more fully in life again. Her energy levels improved, and with the pain subsiding, she could shift her focus from merely surviving to actively healing. Maya's decision to embrace Ayurveda had brought her not just physical relief, but also a renewed sense of hope. It was a turning point that allowed her to reclaim her life, step by step, as her health improved and the burden of pain gradually lifted.

Just as her health seemed to be taking a positive turn with the success of her Ayurvedic treatment, an unexpected setback struck, catching her off guard. One afternoon, after returning from her internship, Maya found herself caught in a sudden, torrential downpour. By the time she reached home, she was completely soaked, chilled to the bone from the cold and wet conditions. She thought little of it at first, simply grateful to be back indoors. But as the evening wore on, she began to feel unwell. Her body, already weakened from the strain of the autoimmune disease and the ongoing transition to Ayurvedic treatments, struggled to cope with the shock from the rain exposure. By the time she settled in for the night, she was burning up with a high fever that seemed to come out of nowhere, she felt helpless and hopeless, once again.

The fever hit her hard and fast, throwing her back into a state of physical distress she hadn't experienced in a while. Her body, already fighting so many battles, now had to contend with this fever. The intensity of the fever left her drained and exhausted, and as she lay in bed, she felt as though the ground beneath her had shifted once again. After making slow and steady progress in managing her joint pain and overall health, this sudden fever was a brutal reminder of her body's vulnerability. It threatened to undo all the positive steps she had taken, casting a shadow over the hope she had begun to feel.

Maya knew this was more than just a simple cold or flu. Her immune system, already compromised, was struggling to fend off the infection. The fever raged on for days, each spike a reminder of how delicate her recovery truly was. Every muscle in her body ached, and her energy, once slowly returning, now seemed to disappear entirely. As the fever persisted, it became clear that this was not just a passing illness, but a significant setback in her journey to healing. The path ahead, which had seemed to be clearing, was once again clouded with uncertainty.

But the fever was just the beginning. As Maya fought the relentless heat of her fever, a far more alarming issue began to surface. Her haemoglobin levels, which had been stabilized for a time after her initial diagnosis and treatment, started to plummet. Day after day, as her fever raged, her blood tests revealed a troubling decline in her haemoglobin count. The red blood cells, crucial for carrying oxygen throughout her body, were disappearing at an alarming rate, much like they had during her initial hospitalization.

The recurrence of this issue brought a deep sense of dread. Maya remembered all too well the harrowing days when her haemoglobin levels had first fallen, when the fatigue had been so overwhelming that she could barely stand. Now, it seemed as though she was reliving that nightmare. Each day brought a new, unsettling drop in her haemoglobin count, signaling that her condition was becoming critical once more. The doctors were concerned, and so was Maya. The rapid decline in her blood levels meant that her body was once again in a precarious state, and she was at risk for serious complications.

This sudden turn of events shook her deeply. After making so much progress, she was once again facing a serious and potentially life-threatening health crisis. The fever, combined with the dangerous drop in her haemoglobin, left her feeling like she was back at square one, battling a foe she thought she had already conquered. It was a test of her resilience—one that left her grappling with fear, frustration, and uncertainty. Maya realized that her journey to recovery was far from over. Instead, it was filled with unexpected hurdles, each one more challenging than the last, and she would need every ounce of strength and determination to navigate through this new storm.

As Maya's health continued to decline, it became increasingly clear that she could no longer manage her condition on her own. The joint pain, the recurring fever, and the dangerous drop in her haemoglobin levels had combined into a critical situation, leaving her no choice but to be hospitalized once again. Unlike her first admission, this time the stakes felt even higher. Not only was she battling a life-threatening illness, but she was also acutely aware of the responsibilities awaiting her outside the hospital walls,which could have been even more difficult to deal with.

She had been in the middle of an important internship, one she had worked hard to secure and that was meant to be a cornerstone of her professional development. Alongside this, she was working on a crucial project for her college, a milestone in her academic career that would significantly impact her future opportunities. Both of these tasks were more than just obligations—they were dreams she had been striving toward, and she knew how much was riding on them. The thought of falling behind, of not being able to complete what she had started, filled her with anxiety and a sense of dread.

Maya was determined to push through, to somehow balance her health and her commitments, but her body had other plans. The illness had taken a severe toll on her, and no matter how strong her will was, she had no choice but to be admitted to the hospital for the second time. This was a sobering reality. Her condition had deteriorated to a point where urgent medical intervention was necessary, and the gravity of the situation was undeniable. The medical team acted swiftly, administering intensive treatment to address her haemoglobin loss, stabilize her autoimmune condition, and restore some semblance of strength to her worn-out body.

For the next week, Maya lay in the hospital bed, battling not only her physical symptoms but also the mental strain of falling behind in her work. As she lay there, surrounded by the hum of hospital machinery and the sterile walls of her room, her thoughts constantly drifted back to her internship and her college project. The deadline for her project was rapidly approaching, and the work she had planned to complete was still unfinished. Her internship, which was a vital component of the project, had been cut short due to her illness, leaving her uncertain about how she would catch up. The weight of this realization pressed heavily on her already fragile state, she felt a deep sense of stress and anxiety. She had come so far in her academic and professional journey, but now, it felt like everything was slipping through her fingers.

However, Maya was not one to give up easily. Even though the overwhelming odds stacked against her, she knew that she couldn't afford to let her illness derail her future. This fight was about more than just her health—it was about reclaiming control over her life and proving to herself that she could overcome even the most daunting challenges. She couldn't allow everything she had worked so hard for to slip away in the fraction of a second because of her illness.Maya sighed softly, murmuring, *"I can't let everything fall apart now... I've worked too hard for this."* With this determination fueling her, she focused on recovering, knowing that if she could stabilize her health, she could still make up for lost time.

The doctors, recognizing her fierce determination and the importance of her academic and professional goals, worked with her to create a treatment plan that would get her back on her feet as quickly as possible. With their support, and with her own inner resolve, Maya began to stabilize. Her haemoglobin levels were slowly brought back to safe levels, her fever broke, and her joint pain became more manageable. After a week of intensive treatment, she was discharged from the hospital. However, she knew that while she was out of immediate danger, the road ahead was still going to be an uphill battle. She had lost valuable time and still had to contend with the effects of her illness, but Maya refused to let that deter her.

Once home, she immediately set her mind to the task of catching up. There were moments of doubt and exhaustion, but Maya drew on every ounce of strength and determination she had left. She reached out to her professors, explaining her situation and requesting extensions where necessary. She reconnected with her internship supervisor, who, understanding the gravity of her circumstances, offered support and flexibility.

Through it all, one of her closest friends stood by her side, helping her day in and day out with her project. Whether it was gathering research, organizing notes, or simply keeping her motivated during the toughest moments, their unwavering support became a lifeline. On days when Maya's fatigue made it nearly impossible to concentrate, her friend patiently went over the material with her, ensuring she stayed on track.

(Maya and Raghav working on the project at Maya's home)

Maya: *(sighs) "I don't know, Raghav. I feel like I'm drowning. I can't concentrate, and I just don't have the energy to keep going."*

Raghav: *(gently) "Maya, I can see you're exhausted, but you're not alone in this. I'm right here with you. We've gotten this far together, and we'll finish it too. Take a break for a moment, but don't give up now."*

Maya: (pauses, shaking her head) "I feel like I'm failing... like I'm just not capable of doing this anymore."

Raghav: (sitting beside her, reassuringly) "You're not failing, Maya. You're just human. And, honestly, there's no one more capable of doing this than you. But remember, strength isn't just about pushing through alone—sometimes it's about leaning on the people who care about you. I'm here. Always."

Maya: (softly, with a faint smile) "I don't know how I would've done this without you. You've been my anchor in all of this. Thank you, Raghav... I think, with you by my side, I can do this."

Raghav: (with a mischievous smile) "Of course you can! But, hey, don't forget—you owe me big time for all this work. You can send me some money whenever you feel like I've done enough. I accept cash, cards, and online payments. I'm not picky!"

This made her smile, the weight of everything momentarily lifted by Raghav's playful humor.

It wasn't just the practical help that mattered, though—it was the silent strength that came with knowing someone believed in her, even when she had lost belief in herself. In life, it's said that a single true friend is worth more than a hundred acquaintances, and she now understood that completely.

It wasn't easy—there were days when the exhaustion from her illness made it difficult to focus, and moments when the sheer amount of work ahead of her seemed insurmountable—but Maya pressed on. With the help of those who cared for her, she refused to let her illness define her or take away the future she had worked so hard for.

She approached her project with renewed vigor, determined not to let this setback define her. Every task she completed, every step she took toward finishing her internship and her project, was a small victory in her larger fight for her future. Maya knew that this was about more than just completing her work—it was about proving to HERSELF that she could rise above the challenges life had thrown at her. Her illness may have disrupted her plans, but it hadn't taken away her resolve. Determined, Maya told herself, *"Every hurdle I cross brings me closer to who I'm meant to be."* She was stronger than she had ever realized, and this fight wasn't just about her education; it was about reclaiming her life and proving her resilience.

In life, every major decision comes with its own cost—a cost that is often hidden in the shadows, only revealing itself once the choice has been made. These big decisions, whether in pursuit of change, growth, or healing, are rarely simple. They demand courage, commitment, and sometimes, sacrifice. When we stand at the crossroads of an important choice, it's easy to focus on the possibilities and the potential outcomes. We may dream of a better future, a solution to our problems, or the fulfillment of our deepest desires. Yet, with every step forward, we must also contend with the realities that come with that decision.

Moreover, big decisions require us to step outside our comfort zones, often pushing us into uncomfortable and unfamiliar territory. There's a price to pay for choosing change over security, for embracing uncertainty over predictability. The fear of failure can haunt us, as can the second-guessing that comes with wondering if we made the right choice.

But while the cost of big decisions can feel overwhelming, they also offer something profound in return: growth. Every sacrifice, every challenge we face on the path we choose, teaches us more about ourselves. We learn resilience in the face of adversity. We discover inner strength we didn't know we had. We begin to understand that the real cost of a big decision is not just in what we give up, but in what we gain along the way—experience, wisdom, and a deeper understanding of who we are and what we are capable of.

Chapter 6 Breaking the cycle

Beneath harsh machines,

Pain and shadows intertwine,

Truth waits in sharp tests.

After her discharge from the hospital, Maya had managed to rebuild her life, finding a way to balance the challenges of her autoimmune disease with her day-to-day activities. She had grown accustomed to managing her joint pain and had adjusted her routine, allowing her to work full-time and maintain a sense of normalcy. With her medications under control and a newfound appreciation for her health, Maya had reached a place where she felt content and happy. Life was moving forward, and she was finally in a good place.

However, after returning from a relaxing trip with friends, Maya suddenly began experiencing an intense stomach ache. Initially, she brushed it off, thinking it was something minor. She visited her family doctor, who prescribed a week-long course of medication. But as the days passed, the pain didn't subside—it grew worse. Despite taking the medicine faithfully, the ache became unbearable, the pain was unbearable—an excruciating, twisting sensation deep in her stomach, as if something inside her was clawing, tearing, refusing to let go. Maya curled up on her bed, clutching her abdomen, her body drenched in sweat despite the cool air in the room.

In the midst of it all, frustration boiled over. *"Why isn't anyone doing anything?!"* she screamed, her voice raw with anger and desperation. Her family rushed to her side, their faces filled with worry, their hands reaching out to comfort her. But nothing they did was enough. *"I'm in pain! Can't you see? You're just standing there!"* she cried, her voice cracking as another wave of pain surged through her.

Her mother held her trembling hand, her father paced anxiously, and her sister hovered nearby, helplessly offering water, painkillers—anything to ease her suffering. But Maya couldn't see their efforts through the haze of her agony. She felt alone in her pain, trapped in a body that was betraying her.

Her family watched, their own hearts breaking, knowing they were doing everything they could—but it still wasn't enough. And Maya, drowning in pain and helplessness, couldn't help but lash out, even though deep down, she knew they were hurting too.

Maya found herself back in the hospital, facing yet another daunting health challenge, just when she thought she had regained control over her life.As the familiar smell of antiseptic filled her senses, Maya realized that fate had something else in store for her. Just as she had begun to rebuild her life, another challenge emerged, knocking her down once more.

Maya had a deep instinct that this time, her recovery would not be a quick one. The severity of the stomach pain felt different, more relentless, and harder to shake it off. With this unsettling feeling gnawing at her, she made the difficult decision to quit her job, choosing to focus entirely on her health. It wasn't an easy choice—Maya had always been dedicated to her work—but she knew that, this time, she had to prioritize herself to avoid any worse outcomes.

Over the course of the next six months, Maya's fears were confirmed. She was admitted to the hospital three times, each stay longer than the last. Each time she left, thinking the worst was over, only for the stomach pain to return with full force just days later. The ache was unrelenting, a constant companion, no matter what she ate—or didn't eat. Maya, frustrated and confused, often found herself asking, *"What's exactly wrong with me? Why am I facing this when I haven't done anything wrong with my diet?"*

The physical toll on her body was undeniable. Already thin as a rail, the continuous bouts of vomiting, pain, and hospital stays caused her to lose an additional 10 kilograms, leaving her looking more frail and gaunt than ever before. The weight loss was rapid and dramatic, and Maya struggled to recognize herself in the mirror. Her once-vibrant face had become pale and lifeless, her cheeks hollow, her eyes dull. She appeared like a shadow of the strong, self-assured woman she had once been.

Maya (staring at her reflection, her fingers tracing the sharp edges of her collarbones): "Is this really me? When did I start looking like this?"

Her Reflection (coldly, unflinching): "You already know the answer."

Maya (scoffing, crossing her arms): "No, I don't. None of this makes sense. I haven't done anything wrong. I eat right, I take care of myself. So why is my body turning against me?"

Her Reflection: "Because this isn't about what you did or didn't do. It's happening whether you want to believe it or not."

Maya (voice shaking, fists clenching at her sides): "No. This shouldn't be happening to me. I've been through enough. I don't deserve this."

Her Reflection (tilting its head, almost amused): "Oh, so that's how it works? You think fairness has anything to do with illness?"

Maya (gritting her teeth, blinking back tears): "I just… I just want to wake up and feel normal. I want to go a day without pain, without being afraid of when it'll come back. I want to stop being weak."

Her Reflection (softening, but still firm): *"You think you're weak?"*

Maya (laughs bitterly): *"Look at me! I can barely eat without getting sick. I've lost so much weight I look like a ghost. I can't even walk for long without feeling like I'll collapse. How is that not weak?"*

Her Reflection (meeting her gaze, unwavering): *"Weak people don't keep fighting. Weak people give up. But you're still here. You're still asking questions. You're still searching for answers."*

Maya (whispering, barely audible): *"Then why does it feel like I'm losing myself?"*

Her Reflection (gently): *"Because you're in the middle of the fight. And the middle is always the hardest part."*

Maya (closing her eyes, exhaling shakily): *"I just want it to stop."*

Her Reflection: *"I know. But for now, you have to keep going, don't you ever give up, Maya, you have got this !"*

(Maya let out a deep breath, her hands gripping the edges of the sink. She didn't have a choice. She would keep going. She had to.)

Maya had always carried herself with confidence. She was known for walking with her head held high, even in the face of adversity. But now, even the simplest tasks—like walking from one room to another—left her feeling utterly drained and worn out. It was as though the life force had been sucked from her, leaving her a shell of the person she used to be.

It's true what they say—"A healthy outside starts from the inside." And as Maya lost her physical strength, the toll it took on her spirit was undeniable. She felt more miserable than ever, not just because of the relentless pain, but because of the overwhelming sense that she was losing herself. This wasn't just about her body failing her; it was about the loss of her identity, her vitality, and the confidence she had always drawn from her inner strength. Now, she was fighting not only the illness, but the fear that she would never again be the woman she once was.

"You can choose courage, or you can choose comfort, but you cannot choose both."

Brene Brown

Even the doctors were baffled by Maya's condition. Every treatment they tried seemed to offer temporary relief, but soon enough, the stomach pain and vomiting would return, as fierce as ever. It wasn't just Maya who was frustrated—the medical team was equally perplexed (and now you too, my dear reader)! They had tried multiple courses of medications and interventions, but none seemed to provide lasting results. The persistence of her symptoms left them questioning what they might be missing. Why wasn't anything working? Why did the pain keep coming back as soon as she left the hospital?

After weeks of trial and error, the doctors realized they needed to dig deeper. The usual tests and treatments weren't getting to the root of the problem. Something more complex was clearly at play, and they couldn't afford to keep sending her home without answers. So, they decided to move forward with more extensive diagnostic tests, hoping to finally uncover what was going wrong inside Maya's body.

A CT scan was ordered to get a clearer picture of her abdomen and see if there was any structural issue contributing to her pain. Along with the scan, they scheduled an endoscopy to take a closer look at her stomach and digestive tract.

As Maya lay in the hospital, hooked up to IVs and surrounded by the sterile beeping of machines, the reality of her situation began to sink in. She was no longer just battling a mysterious illness—she was in a race to uncover what had gone so wrong inside her body.

The situation took a sharp turn for the worse during Maya's CT scan, a moment that would become etched in her memory as one of the most humiliating and unbearable experiences of her medical journey.

As part of the procedure, she was given an injection to enhance the scan's visibility. But instead of the smooth process she had anticipated, her body reacted violently. Without warning, a surge of nausea overtook her, and before she could stop it, she vomited—right there, inside the confined space of the machine.

The thick, acidic liquid splattered onto her face, clinging to her hair, soaking her gown, and trickling down her neck onto the cold surface beneath her. The warmth of it against her skin made her stomach lurch again. The stench, the sensation—it was suffocating. She gagged, her body shaking with disgust, her mind screaming at her to get out, to run to the nearest sink, to wipe away the filth that now coated her.

Panic set in as she tried to move, her instinct screaming for her to escape the wretched feeling crawling all over her skin. But before she could sit up, a firm voice from the monitoring room echoed through the intercom.

"Maya, please stay still. Moving now will disrupt the scan."

Stay still? How could she?

Her entire body felt defiled, her dignity crushed beneath the weight of her helplessness. She wanted to scream, to claw at the mess on her skin and rid herself of the sticky, disgusting sensation. But she was trapped— trapped in the sterile, mechanical confines of the CT machine, with the unrelenting hum drilling and the acrid taste of bile still lingering in her mouth.

Every poke, every prod, every humiliating moment of this illness had pushed her further into a world where she had no control. And now, lying there covered in her own sickness, unable to do anything but endure, she felt an overwhelming sense of helplessness that nearly broke her.

The medical staff rushed to her aid as soon as the scan was complete, offering apologies and hurried words of comfort, but it didn't matter.

The damage was done.

Unfortunately, this was only one of many difficult moments. Maya's experience with an endoscopy before being hospitalized for her stomach infection had been relatively smooth. Back then, she had been given anesthesia, allowing her to drift into a state where the procedure was nothing more than a blurry, dreamlike memory. But this time, things were different. There was no anesthesia to dull the sensations, no hazy fog to mask the reality of what was happening.In fact, the moment they tried to give her the pipe for anesthesia through her nose, Maya, in her usual defiant fashion, decided it was more "uncomfortable" than anything else and pulled it out. As a result, she wasn't asleep during the process, and suddenly, everything felt way too real. At that moment, Maya wondered if she'd made a "tiny" mistake.

Fully conscious and aware, Maya felt every sensation, every movement of the instruments inside her body. She could see the medical staff working around her, hear the clinks of the instruments, and feel the discomfort that came with the procedure. It was an altogether more intense and unsettling experience than before. *"I can do this... just breathe,"* she kept telling herself, trying to stay focused and composed as the procedure went on.

But even in the midst of such anxiety, Maya found an unexpected source of strength. Maya turned inward to the one thing that had always brought her solace— her prayers.As her trembling hands clutched the hospital sheets, she began to pray quietly, seeking some semblance of peace amid the chaos.

The tests were executed while she remained under close observation, each day feeling longer and more grueling than the last.For Maya, the waiting was the hardest part. The uncertainty gnawed at her as she lay in that hospital bed, day after day. She couldn't help but feel a growing sense of dread—*"what if they still couldn't figure it out? What if this endless cycle of pain and brief respite continued?"*

As the tests were completed and the doctors pored over the results, Maya knew that the next step would be critical. She had already been through so much, and now, everything depended on whether these new tests would finally provide the answers she so desperately needed.

After days of confusion, and countless tests, the results finally pointed to a startling conclusion—Maya's debilitating stomach pain and relentless vomiting were being caused by a side effect of the very medicine she had been taking for the past three years to manage her autoimmune condition. The discovery was both shocking and frustrating. The medication that had once brought her relief, enabling her to function and reclaim some normalcy in her life, was now the root cause of her severe gastrointestinal issues.

It was a difficult realization for Maya to accept. The medicine had been a cornerstone of her treatment, something she had relied on as a lifeline in managing her autoimmune disease. But now, that same medicine was slowly damaging her small intestine, leading to the unrelenting stomach ache and frequent vomiting that had disrupted her life so intensely in recent months.

The gastrointestinal team, after reviewing her condition in detail, explained that continuing the medication would only cause further harm to her digestive system. The damage to her small intestine was evident, and they warned that if the treatment wasn't stopped immediately, the consequences could become even more severe. Armed with this information, they reached out to her autoimmune specialist, the doctor who had been overseeing her care for years.

When the decision was made, it marked a pivotal moment in her journey. The medication she had trusted for years was now being pulled from her treatment plan, leaving her feeling both relieved and anxious. On one hand, discontinuing the medicine offered hope that her stomach pain might finally subside, but on the other, she was faced with the uncertainty of how to manage her autoimmune disease without it.

Discontinuing the medication was a leap of faith, a step into the unknown. Would the pain stop? Would her autoimmune condition worsen without it? These were the questions that haunted her as she prepared to take this new path.

As Maya took her first steps without the medication that had been part of her daily routine for so long, she couldn't help but feel a glimmer of hope mixed with trepidation. It was the beginning of another chapter in her ongoing fight for her health, one filled with uncertainty but also the possibility of relief after months of suffering.

Maya's mother (hesitantly, watching her daughter closely): *"Maya… do you ever feel like your autoimmune doctor is to blame for all of this? I mean, they prescribed the medication for three years, and now we find out it's been damaging your stomach all along."*

Maya (shaking her head, a tired smile playing on her lips): *"No, Ma. I don't see the doctor as a culprit."*

Maya's mother (frowning, concerned): *"But beta, they gave you something that made things worse. If they had known—"*

Maya (interrupting softly): *"If they had known, they wouldn't have given it to me, Ma. That medicine helped control my autoimmune disease for years. It wasn't meant to harm me—it just… it just turned out this way."*

Maya's mother (voice heavy with emotion): *"But why you? Why did this happen to you?"*

Maya (letting out a small, bitter laugh): "That's the question, isn't it? Why me? Why did this medication affect me like this when so many others take it without any issues? Why did my stomach have to suffer? Why did I have to go through all this pain?"

She paused for a moment, staring off into the distance as if searching for an answer she already knew.

Maya (softly, but with conviction): "Because it was in my destiny."

Her mother's eyes welled up with tears, but Maya reached for her hand, squeezing it gently.

Maya (continuing): "This was meant to happen to me. Maybe to test me, maybe to teach me something, I don't know. But blaming the doctor won't change anything. They did what they thought was best. The rest… it was just written in my fate."

Maya's mother (wiping her tears): "You're stronger than I ever realized, beta."

Maya (smirking, trying to lighten the mood): "I have to be, Ma. I don't really have a choice, do I?"

(Her mother gave her a sad, knowing smile. She wished she could take away her daughter's pain, rewrite her fate. But in that moment, she also realized—

Maya wasn't just surviving this battle. She was facing it head-on, with resilience that even pain couldn't break.)

Chapter 7 A Blessing in Disguise

Storm clouds hide the light,

Yet a silver glow breaks through,

Blessings in disguise.

After discontinuing the medication that had wreaked havoc on her stomach, Maya was cautiously hopeful that things would begin to stabilize. Her body had been through so much, and she clung to the hope that without the harmful medication, she could start rebuilding her health. However, her autoimmune specialist wasn't ready to leave anything to chance. After a few weeks of careful monitoring, the specialist suggested it was time to run some additional tests to ensure that discontinuing the medication hadn't caused any further damage to her body.

Maya, still emotionally and physically drained from the months of suffering, agreed, understanding the importance of staying vigilant. She had learned the hard way that when it came to her health, nothing could be left unchecked. The specialist ordered a series of blood and urine tests, wanting to examine whether her organs had been affected or if her autoimmune condition had flared up again in another part of her body.

A few days later, one of the test results came back abnormal. It was her kidney function report, which showed an alarming level of protein in her urine—far beyond the normal standards. This finding couldn't be ignored. High levels of protein in the urine, known as proteinuria, often signaled that the kidneys were under strain or being damaged in some way. The specialist feared that Maya's kidneys might be the next casualty of her complex medical situation.

The doctors, taking no chances, quickly advised Maya that she needed to be hospitalized again—this time for a kidney biopsy. The procedure would allow them to take a small sample of her kidney tissue to analyze what was causing the elevated protein levels. The biopsy would provide the answers they desperately needed to understand if her kidneys were being attacked by her autoimmune disease, or if the medication had left lasting damage.

Maya, though exhausted by yet another health scare, agreed to the hospitalization. She had learned to brace herself for whatever came next, but this latest development left her shaken. The thought that her kidneys, such a vital part of her body, might be compromised filled her with fear. *"How much more can my body take?"* she thought, staring at the hospital walls that had become all too familiar. She couldn't help but wonder if this battle was ever going to end.

When she was admitted for the two-day hospital stay, the doctors explained the biopsy procedure in detail. They needed to understand exactly what was happening inside her kidneys, and the biopsy was the most direct way to gather that information. The waiting that followed was excruciating for Maya, would she be able to endure the pain again?The uncertainty of what the procedure would bring left her wondering how it would all end up for her.

On the day of her kidney biopsy, Maya went through the procedure where a small tissue sample had to be taken from her kidney. During the biopsy, she wasn't given full anaesthesia; instead, only the specific part of her body where the sample was to be taken was numbed. She was awake the entire time and could see the biopsy being performed. She could even feel the sensation of blood flowing from the area around her stomach. Although she didn't experience any pain, the feeling of blood flowing was deeply unsettling and frightening for her.

She prayed silently, hoping that the biopsy would reveal something they could treat—something that could be fixed before it became irreversible. But deep down, the fear lingered: what if this was yet another long road she would have to walk, another battle she wasn't prepared for?

After the biopsy was completed, the doctors were firm in their instructions to Maya. She needed to have someone with her at all times, no matter what—even if it was just to go to the bathroom. This was crucial to her recovery, especially given the risks involved following the procedure. Maya, who always stood diligent in whichever decision she made, understood the importance of these precautions and made sure to follow them closely. Every movement required extra care now, and she didn't take any chances.

When she needed to go to the bathroom, Maya asked her mother to accompany her, just as the doctor had advised. Everything seemed normal at first, but as she stood there with her mother by her side, an unexpected wave of dizziness washed over her. It hit suddenly, and Maya instinctively reached out to her mother for support. But before she could steady herself or say a word, her body gave in—her vision blurred, and she collapsed into unconsciousness.

Her mother, startled but quick to react, managed to catch her just as Maya's body went limp. Her father, rushing to the scene, helped support Maya as they carefully carried her back to the hospital bed. As they laid her down, Maya slowly began to regain consciousness, but the last few moments were a complete void. For 15 to 20 seconds, she had no memory of what had just occurred. Her mind was a blur, and the only thing she could grasp was the reality that she had fainted.

It was a terrifying moment for Maya and her family. The sudden loss of control over her own body was unsettling, and it only deepened the sense of vulnerability she had been feeling since her health had begun to spiral. Her parents, ever vigilant, stayed close by her side, ensuring she was safe as she slowly recovered from the dizzy spell. For Maya, this episode was yet another reminder of just how fragile her body had become, and how carefully she needed to navigate the road ahead.

After the biopsy, the doctors planned a course of treatment based on the results. Initially, there was a plan to administer a specific injection as part of her treatment. Although the injection was relatively inexpensive, it was expected to have a strong impact on her body, potentially causing significant side effects.

The results of Maya's kidney biopsy came back with an unexpected but deeply welcome surprise—they were normal. What had initially appeared to be a serious and concerning kidney issue turned out to be nothing more than a scare. This fortunate outcome spared her from further invasive treatments, including the potentially harmful injection the doctors had planned, which could have taken a heavy toll on her already fragile body.

When the news arrived, the relief was palpable. The doctors themselves were taken aback. They had been almost certain that Maya's kidneys were compromised, which is why they had recommended the biopsy in the first place. Everything had pointed toward an underlying problem, and they had fully expected the results to confirm their suspicions. But instead, the normal biopsy results provided a rare moment of relief in what had been a long, grueling journey.

Maya's mother, who had been by her side throughout, was overcome with emotion. Through tears of gratitude, she whispered, *"This is truly a blessing in disguise."* What could have been a life-altering health crisis had turned into a mere scare, and the weight of that realization filled the entire family with profound thankfulness. They knew how easily the situation could have been much worse.

Even though the biopsy had caused Maya significant pain and discomfort, the family chose not to dwell on the procedure itself or the difficulties it had brought. Instead, they focused on the positive—the fact that Maya's kidneys were healthy, and the looming threat of a more severe diagnosis had been lifted. In a moment where it would have been easy to feel frustration toward the doctors for what now seemed like an unnecessary test, they instead chose to express gratitude.

For Maya and her family, the normal biopsy results felt like a miracle, a testament to the power of prayers and faith. What had once seemed like the beginning of another exhausting chapter in her medical journey was now behind her. They were grateful to have faced only a minor inconvenience rather than the major health crisis they had feared, and Maya emerged from the experience with a renewed sense of hope and resilience.

"If the only prayer you ever say in your entire life is thank you, it will be enough."

Meister Eckhart

Chapter 8 Echoes of Silence

Dark clouds fill her mind,

Heavy thoughts weigh down her soul,

Silent battles rage.

After being discharged from the hospital, Maya returned home to focus on her recovery. The stomach ache had subsided, but the toll it had taken on her body was evident. She had lost a significant amount of weight during her hospital stay, and now, she faced the difficult task of rebuilding her strength. Eating was no longer just about nourishment; it had become a daily battle as she struggled to regain the weight she had lost. Despite her efforts, progress felt slow, and the reflection in the mirror served as a constant reminder of how frail she had become. Physically, she was mending, but the emotional and mental strain of her journey had only just begun to surface.

Her mind seemed to be stuck in a rut, and for the first time in her journey, she was unsure how she would make it through, endlessly revolving around a single thought, a side effect of the medicines she was prescribed. Although these medications worked wonders for her physical health, and to gain weight, they took a toll on her mental well-being. Each dose seemed to tie her mind into knots, making it difficult to focus on anything else. Instead, she would latch onto one idea, chewing it over and over, replaying it in her head like a broken record.

She constantly felt useless, as if she were just a shadow of her former self. Not working, not studying, not doing anything productive—these repetitive thoughts of worthlessness haunted her day and night. The sadness it brought was overwhelming, pulling her deeper into a cycle of negative thinking, leaving her feeling trapped and unable to break free from her own mind.

Maya (lying in bed, staring at the ceiling, her voice laced with frustration): *"What am I even doing with my life?"*

Her Thoughts (whispering, persistent): *"Nothing. You're doing nothing. You used to have goals, ambitions and what not, Maya. Now, look at you."*

Maya (clenching her fists, swallowing hard): *"It's not like I chose this? I didn't ask for this pain, for this illness, did I?"*

Her Thoughts (mockingly): *"And yet, here you are. No job. No studies. No purpose. Just existing."*

Maya (sitting up abruptly, gripping her blanket): *"That's not fair! I want to work, I want to be productive. But how can I, when I can barely get through a day without feeling like my body is betraying me?"*

Her Thoughts (coldly): *"Excuses. Other people push through. Other people keep going. Why can't you?"*

Maya (voice breaking, eyes welling up with tears): *"Because I'm tired! I'm exhausted, mentally and* *physically. It's not just about pushing through—it's about survival at this point."*

Her Thoughts (challenging): *"So, what? You're just going to sit here forever, wasting away, while the world moves on without you?"*

Maya (whispering, defeated): *"I don't know…"*

The next stage of kubler ross theory:- **DEPRESSION**

For two long and exhausting months, Maya was engulfed in a deep depression that seemed impossible to escape. Despite her best efforts to lift herself out of the darkness, these thoughts held her tightly in its grip. Each day felt like a heavy burden, with an overwhelming sense of hopelessness weighing her down. The simple act of getting out of bed in the morning became a monumental challenge, as she couldn't find a single reason to face the day ahead.

Instead, she found solace in sleep, retreating from the world for hours on end. Sleep was her only escape, a way to temporarily numb the pain and silence the thoughts that tormented her. The more she slept, the more disconnected she became from reality. Her days blurred into nights, with no distinction between the two, as time seemed to lose all meaning.

Without any work or responsibilities to anchor her, her life felt empty and purposeless. The lack of structure only intensified her feelings of worthlessness and despair. She was adrift in a sea of misery, with no clear direction or hope for the future.

As the days dragged on, she could feel herself unravelling, her mind slowly slipping away as the depression consumed her completely. Maya often found herself overwhelmed by waves of sadness that seemed to come out of nowhere, leaving her in tears whenever she was alone. The solitude amplified her grief, making it feel as though the walls were closing in on her. She would cry silently in the privacy of her room, feeling the weight of her emotions pressing down on her, with no clear way to release the pain she was carrying inside.

"A greater woman has faith, but even statues crumble if they're made to wait."

Taylor Swift

But her tears weren't confined to moments of solitude. Even in the presence of her parents, she couldn't hold back the flood of emotions. Despite their best efforts to reassure her, she felt a profound sense of despair that she couldn't shake off. Her tears flowed freely in their presence, a visible expression of the grief that she couldn't articulate in words.

*"One day, your actions will stand right before you —
just don't be shocked when they demand their due."*

-Unknown

Maya had always prided herself on her ability to speak
her mind, an attribute that had defined her since she
was a child. Her honesty was direct, sharp, and
unfiltered. While many admired her for it, seeing her as
someone untouched by the pretenses of the world,
others found themselves hurt by her words, often
unintentionally. Maya herself rarely stopped to consider
the impact of her bluntness. To her, truth was an
absolute — something that should be told, regardless of
how it made others feel.

She had heard somewhere, perhaps in passing, that
words have the power to both heal and harm. But Maya
had never truly understood the weight of those words
until now. Looking back, she wondered if the seeds she
had sown in her past — be it in this life or a previous
one — were finally bearing bitter fruit. Had she, in her
relentless pursuit of truth, hurt someone deeply? Maybe
not through actions, but with words that left invisible
scars. The realization struck her hard: the wounds she
had caused weren't external, but buried within the
hearts of those she had spoken to so freely.

In her life, Maya had wielded honesty like a sword,
sharp and unyielding. She had seen it as a virtue, a

mark of purity in a world tainted by deceit. Yet, in time, she came to understand that the world doesn't always see bluntness as innocence. People clung to the bitterness of her words, not the truth she intended. They didn't grasp the purity of her intentions; all they felt was the sting.

Maya had never stopped to reflect on this. It wasn't that she meant to harm anyone — on the contrary, she believed that honesty was the highest form of respect one could offer. But she failed to realize that it was not just about being right, it was about being kind. Her words had power, and that power, when unchecked, could leave more wounds than healing. *"The truth may be bitter, but the tongue need not be,"* she had once heard, yet never understood. Honesty didn't have to be sharp; it could be delivered with softness, with compassion. This was a lesson she had never learned.

Now, in the present, Maya found herself ensnared by the weight of her own thoughts, her mind a dark and empty well. For the first time in her life, the words that had once flowed so freely failed her. Her thoughts, once sharp and relentless, were silent. No matter how hard she tried, she couldn't articulate a single coherent idea.

She sat in that silence, struggling to understand. And then, as if the emptiness itself had formed into a voice, she heard something—her own thoughts speaking back to her. But this time, they weren't sharp or relentless. They were different. Softer.

Maya: *[Whispering to herself, gripping her arms] Is this my punishment? Is this how God balances the scales? I spoke too much, too carelessly… and now I have nothing left to say.*

Maya's Voice: *[Softly, from within] Perhaps it's not a punishment, but a lesson.*

Maya: *[Scoffs] A lesson? What kind of lesson is this? My mind used to be sharp, quick. I never struggled to find words. Now, there's just… emptiness. It's like my own thoughts have abandoned me.*

Maya's Voice: *[Calmly] Or maybe, they've been silenced so you can hear something else.*

Maya: *Hear what? The regret? The echoes of every word I threw like a blade? I didn't mean to hurt anyone. I was just… honest.*

Maya's Voice: *[Gently] And do you think honesty is only about speaking the truth?*

Maya: *[Pauses] Isn't it? If something is true, it should be said. It's better than lying, better than pretending.*

Maya's Voice: *[Firmly] Better for whom? For you? Or for them?*

Maya: *[Breath hitching, whispering] I never thought about that. I thought truth was a gift. That people should appreciate it. But… they didn't, did they?*

Maya's Voice: *[Softly] No, they didn't. They felt the weight of your words, but not the purity of your intent. They felt the sting, not the wisdom.*

Maya: *[Tears forming, voice trembling] Then… maybe I deserve this. Maybe that's why I have no thoughts left. So I can't hurt anyone anymore.*

Maya's Voice: *[Sighing] Do you really think God is punishing you?*

Maya: *[Looking down, whispering] If this isn't punishment, then what is it? I feel empty. My mind, my words, my voice… they're all gone.*

Maya's Voice: *[Gently] Maybe it's not emptiness. Maybe it's space. Space for something new.*

Maya: *[Looking up slowly] Something new?*

Maya's Voice: *[Nods] Understanding. Reflection. Growth. You always filled the silence with words, never allowing yourself to sit in it, to listen. Maybe this is not the end of your voice, but the beginning of a softer one.*

Maya: *[Eyes widening slightly] A softer voice…*

***Maya's Voice:** [Encouraging] Yes. One that doesn't wield truth like a sword, but offers it like a light. One that doesn't seek to wound, but to heal.*

***Maya:** [Takes a deep breath, feeling something shift within her] I don't know if I can do that.*

***Maya's Voice:** [Smiling] You don't have to know. You just have to try.*

For Maya, this moment of realization was both terrifying and humbling. She had always believed in the righteousness of her actions, but now she saw the cost of her truth-telling. It wasn't enough to be right; one had to be kind as well. As she stood at the edge of this realization, she understood that words, though intangible, carried immense weight. They could build bridges or burn them. And in her life, she had unknowingly set fire to many.

When her friends visited, hoping to lift her spirits and bring some light into her life, she still couldn't escape the sadness. They laughed, shared stories of their daily routines, and reminisced about the good old days. But Maya? She barely spoke. The Maya who used to be the life of every gathering, the one who always had a tale to tell, was now a silent observer. She only managed a faint smile here and there, a hollow reflection of the vibrant person she once was.

"What's the point of being called into these conversations when I have nothing to share?" she thought to herself. There was a time when she would be the center of attraction, drawing everyone in with her wit and stories filled with wisdom. But now, the very thought of being in the spotlight makes her uncomfortable. *"I wish they wouldn't call on me, wouldn't ask me anything,"* she thought quietly. I have nothing to offer, no words, no stories, just this emptiness.

The days of the week seemed to blend into a gray, monotonous blur. When someone asked her, *"How was your week?"* Maya had no answer. All she could say was that she had been at home, with her parents, doing nothing of significance. Her days were spent in a state of limbo, where 'healing' meant simply staying home, doing little more than applying for jobs on her phone, and waiting-hoping-for a reply that might bring a change to her stagnant routine.When people yearn for a daily routine, here Maya was, already exhausted of a life which was full of a fixed routine and no spontaneity.

A situation that seems tragic or insurmountable to one person might be seen by another as an opportunity for growth, change, or new beginnings. It suggests that our mindset and attitude play a significant role in how we perceive and respond to challenges.

For instance, a person who loses a job might initially see it as a devastating event, a tragedy that disrupts their life. However, another individual in the same situation might view it as a chance to explore new career paths, start a business, or pursue a passion that they never had time for before. The loss, while difficult, becomes a doorway to something new and potentially better.

The key idea here is that tragedy and opportunity are often two sides of the same coin. What makes the difference is how we choose to see and respond to the situation, it all depends on our vision. If we focus solely on the loss or difficulty, it can feel overwhelming and hopeless. But if we look for the possibilities that lie within the challenge, we can find ways to turn adversity into something positive and transformative.

This perspective(looking for the brighter side) encourages resilience and optimism, suggesting that even in our darkest moments, there can be hidden opportunities waiting to be discovered, just like Maya's story. It's about finding the silver lining, even in the most difficult circumstances, and using those experiences to grow and create new paths forward.

People who are upbeat tend to have a growth mindset. They believe that challenges and failures are opportunities to learn and grow rather than insurmountable obstacles. They see setbacks as temporary and believe that they have control over their future through their actions and choices.

On the other hand, those who are consistently miserable often have a fixed mindset. They may believe that their circumstances are unchangeable and that they have little control over their lives. This can lead to a sense of helplessness and resignation.

Maya felt an overwhelming sense of vulnerability as she compared herself to her friends, who were all either working or studying, actively engaged in something meaningful. Meanwhile, she was lying in bed, feeling unproductive and burdened by sadness. The contrast between their busy lives and her own inactivity made her feel even more isolated and alone.

Despite being surrounded by her family members, who were constantly by her side, and friends who visited her daily to offer their support, she couldn't shake the feeling of loneliness. Their visits, instead of comforting her, only served as a reminder that they were moving forward with their lives while she was stuck, unable to do anything. The support they offered felt hollow to her, emphasizing the gap between their abilities and her own limitations.

Her physical condition only deepened her sense of helplessness. Her body was so weak that she couldn't manage even the simplest tasks on her own. Every day, Maya had to rely on her mother to help her with basic activities, tasks that once seemed effortless. This dependency made her feel even more unsupported and deeply saddened. She longed for the independence she once had, but her current state made her feel as though she was a burden, adding to her feelings of despair and inadequacy.

Maya came to understand that it was truly her mother's prayers that had spared her from what could have been a devastating outcome. The doctors had made it clear that had her condition not been addressed in time, it could have escalated to the point where she would have needed intensive care in the ICU. While she was grateful for the medical treatment she received, she knew that her recovery was also deeply intertwined with the power of her mother's steadfast prayers and unwavering love.

Her mother's faith in God had been a source of strength throughout this ordeal, and it became evident that this faith had played a significant role in her survival. This experience deepened her appreciation for her mother's devotion and reinforced her belief in the power of faith and prayer. The close brush with tragedy made her realize how much she owed to her mother's unshakeable belief in God's protection, which had guided her through this challenging time.

Our beliefs: We often think of our family as a permanent and unchanging part of our lives, believing that our home is a place where we belong, filled with love and attachment. However, in a deeper, spiritual sense, these relationships and attachments might be seen differently. From this perspective, our family and home are not just about love and belonging but are actually arenas where we are meant to balance out our karmic accounts. Just like in a relationship between a customer and a seller, where one person gives and the other receives, our interactions with family members can be viewed as exchanges-each person playing a role in helping the other fulfil their karmic obligations.

This means that the relationships we hold so dearly are, at their core, opportunities for us to settle the debts of our past actions, to give and receive in ways that lead to spiritual growth and resolution.

Maya's mother exemplifies how we often find ourselves fulfilling karmic obligations from past lives, working through the lessons and relationships that lead to spiritual balance and growth.

Chapter 9 The Weight of Shadows

Trembling but resolved,

She steps toward the healing path,

Finding light in the darkness

When illness forces someone to step away from their work or daily routine, the challenge becomes even more personal. The loss of productivity or independence can feel as difficult as the physical symptoms themselves. Identity becomes tangled with the illness, and the person may find themselves wondering who they are without the strength or vitality they once had. It's a battle not only for health but for a sense of self that seems to slip further away with each setback.

For many, the path to healing involves more than just medicine or treatment; it requires a profound inner strength, a willingness to adapt, and the ability to confront fears of the unknown. It demands resilience in the face of frustration, courage in the midst of vulnerability, and faith that the right solution will eventually emerge, even when the present feels overwhelming.

Maya wasn't one to be easily broken or defeated. For most of her life, she had managed to maintain a balance — facing challenges head-on without letting them drown her. It was during one such time that she realized the stark truth: it was nearly impossible to always remain positive, happy, and carefree.

She began to question everything — her actions, her words, her decisions — and found herself trapped in a cycle of overthinking. No matter how much she tried, she couldn't shake the feeling of being engulfed by her own thoughts (the medicines effect).

But, was she weak ? No. She had never been weak. She had never been weak. In fact, she had always been the one her friends turned to in their moments of despair. She had a way of listening deeply, offering the right words of comfort, and guiding those she loved through their storms. Her friends often sought her out when they were feeling low, knowing that Maya had a way of restoring hope when it felt like the world was closing in. Whether it was a late-night chat or a coffee shop conversation, Maya was the one who held the space for others to unravel their fears and sadness. She had a gift for seeing the silver lining, for showing people the light at the end of their tunnel.At times, all a person needs is an ear to hear and things start falling back to their place, again. Reviving the hopes that were once lost and resuming the life that, once, was meant to be lived, and not just survived.

The weight of her thoughts was immense, and despite knowing that her friends would listen, she couldn't bring herself to reach out. How could she, the one who always knew what to say, admit that now she had no words of comfort for her own self?

As she navigated this difficult period, Maya came to understand that her mind was not solely her own in those moments. The medicines she had been taking — prescribed to help her with a separate issue — had side effects that weighed heavily on her mental state. One of those side effects was the tendency to overthink, to dwell on the same thoughts again and again, spiraling into sadness with no escape in sight.

The realization hit her hard. It wasn't that she had suddenly lost her strength or that life had broken her spirit. It was the medicine. The chemicals that were supposed to help her had an unintended consequence — they clouded her mind, forcing her to relive the same worries and doubts over and over.

One day, Maya found herself standing in front of the mirror, her reflection staring back at her with a mix of vulnerability and determination. She took a deep breath, her voice barely above a whisper, and said, *"I wanted this. I needed a physical reminder of those dark days when I felt like I was drowning in sadness, fragile and exposed."* That day, cutting her hair wasn't about fashion or trends; it was an act of defiance, a deliberate choice to take control in a moment when everything around her felt chaotic and overwhelming. It was a small decision, but to Maya, it symbolized much more—

a reclamation of power when life had left her feeling powerless.

Choosing a style that didn't suit her was intentional, a conscious act of making her internal struggles visible to the world. She wasn't looking for compliments or approval. In fact, she knew the haircut didn't flatter her, but that was precisely the point. *"This isn't about looking good,"* she thought, *"It's about remembering. It's about marking this chapter of my life, like carving my name into a tree, each ring telling a story."* But to her surprise, the people around her had a very different reaction. Her friends and family members began complimenting her on the new look. *"You look amazing,"* they would say, or *"That style really suits you!"*

Maya would smile, nodding politely, but inside, she doubted their words. She thought to herself that maybe they were just being nice, offering empty praise to lift her spirits. She knew the truth—this haircut wasn't meant to be stylish or flattering.

To Maya, the haircut symbolized something much deeper—a visible scar, a scar she wanted to be scripted on her skin, a scar she wanted to revisit whenever she'd go back to this moment - this moment of emptiness and helplessness, while smiling again at herself as she was reminded that how she conquered it all when she literally saw no way out at that point of time, a symbol of the pain she had endured, a reminder that she had walked through the fire and come out the other side. She didn't want to forget these days of emotional turmoil. The unsatisfactory haircut would serve as a constant reminder of the battle she had fought, of the storm she had survived.

Every time she caught a glimpse of herself in a mirror, she would remember the moments when she felt like she was unraveling, the nights filled with tears, the days she had to push through when it felt like the weight of the world was on her shoulders. The haircut was more than a reflection of a passing mood—it was a deliberate mark of survival. It wasn't about hiding her pain or putting on a brave face. It was about acknowledging it, embracing it, and wearing it openly for the world to see.

For Maya, this wasn't an act of self-pity; it was an act of courage. She knew that sometimes the hardest thing wasn't to move past the pain but to face it head-on. She wasn't interested in pretending that everything was fine. Instead, she chose to confront her emotions, to stare down the sadness every day, and to remind herself that, even in her most vulnerable moments, she had the strength to endure. The imperfect haircut was her way of blending with the wind, like the tallest trees that sway but do not break in the face of the storm.

Maya's journey toward healing was not linear. For someone who had always prided herself on her inner strength and resilience, admitting that she could no longer shoulder the burden alone was one of the hardest realizations she ever faced. The weight of her struggles had become too heavy, and no amount of willpower or solitary reflection seemed enough to lift it.

Maya began to understand that seeking professional help wasn't just an option—it was a necessity. After much soul-searching, she made the decision to pursue therapy, recognizing it as a crucial step in reclaiming her sense of self.

For Maya, deciding to go to therapy wasn't the only challenge. Sharing this decision with her parents was a source of deep anxiety. She hesitated, fearing they might not understand her need for professional help. In her mind, the fear lingered that they would see her decision as a sign of weakness, or worse, as an indication that they had somehow failed her. Maya didn't want them to question their own efforts in supporting her, nor did she want them to feel that she had let them down.

But the truth was, therapy wasn't about weakness or failure. It was a step towards healing, growth, and self-awareness. Therapy could be a space for Maya to better understand herself, not because she was broken, but because she was learning to navigate the complexities of life. Seeking help was an act of strength, not a sign of fragility. It could be an investment in her well-being, a decision to take control of her mental health just as one would care for physical health—through regular check-ups, treatments, and preventative measures.

Maya knew that many people still carried the belief that therapy was only for those in extreme crisis or deep trauma, but that simply wasn't true. Therapy could be a tool for anyone who wanted to live a more balanced, mindful life, to work through challenges, or to gain clarity in the midst of confusion. It was a way to build resilience and emotional intelligence, a means of cultivating inner peace.

Yet, as her struggles deepened, Maya knew she had to prioritize her own well-being. **Therapy wasn't a luxury; it was a lifeline.** One evening, after days of rehearsing the words in her head, she finally gathered the courage to speak to her parents about it. Her voice trembled as she shared her decision, bracing herself for their reaction.

Maya: [Nervously] "Mom… Dad… I need to talk to you about something."

Mom: [Looking up, concerned] "Of course. What is it?"

Dad: *[Setting down his newspaper] "You look nervous, Maya. Is everything okay?"*

Maya: *[Swallowing hard, staring at her hands] "I've been struggling… for a while now. And I've decided—I think I need to start therapy."*

Dad: *[Leaning forward] "You're saying this like you expect us to be upset. Why would we be?"*

Maya: *[Hesitates, looking between them] "I don't know… I guess I was scared you might think I'm weak. Or that… maybe you'd feel like you failed me somehow."*

Mom: *[Eyes widening] "Failed you? Maya, no. Not at all. We would never think that."*

Dad: *[Firmly, shaking his head] "Not for a second. If anything, I think it's incredibly strong of you to recognize that you need help and actually do something about it."*

Maya: *"So… you don't, you don't think I'm overreacting? That I should just deal with it on my own?"*

Mom: *"Of course not. Therapy isn't about weakness, Maya. It's about taking care of yourself. It's about finding the right tools to help you through the hard days."*

To her immense surprise and overwhelming relief, Maya's parents responded with nothing but empathy and understanding. Far from viewing her choice as a failure, they acknowledged the courage it took to admit she needed help. They didn't see therapy as a sign of fragility but as a positive, proactive step toward healing. Rather than questioning their own support, they expressed gratitude that she was choosing to confront her struggles head-on. Her parents' acceptance and encouragement marked a turning point in her journey— she felt validated, supported, and understood.

With their blessing, Maya began attending therapy once a week. Each session became a sanctuary, a safe space where she could unravel the thoughts and emotions that had weighed her down for so long. Her therapist helped her explore the depths of her mind with gentle guidance, equipping her with tools and strategies to navigate the turbulent waters of her emotions. In therapy, Maya confronted not only her present struggles but also the memories and patterns from her past that had shaped her.

When the weight of life becomes unbearable, when emotions spiral out of control, or when trauma leaves scars too deep to manage alone, therapy offers something essential: **HOPE**. It provides the tools to navigate through the fog of pain, confusion, or overwhelming sadness. In the quiet of a therapist's office, amid the safety of non-judgmental listening, there is space for honesty—for confronting the thoughts and feelings that are too heavy to bear in isolation.

It's in therapy that many people find their first taste of understanding, a guide through the darkness when they feel lost and alone. It's a place where healing doesn't happen all at once, but through slow, deliberate steps toward self-awareness and acceptance. Each session is a thread, weaving a safety net that keeps them from falling deeper into despair. It's where burdens are lightened, piece by piece, and where the seemingly impossible task of coping with life's hardships becomes manageable.

For those who feel as though they are drowning in their own emotions, therapy becomes the lifeline that pulls them back from the brink. It's not a cure-all, but it offers something vital: perspective, coping mechanisms, and the belief that things can get better, even when it feels like the world is closing in.

Therapy is not a luxury because mental health is not a luxury. It's as fundamental as physical health, deserving of the same care and attention. It is the space where people are reminded that they don't have to carry their struggles alone, that there is support available, and that healing—however slow and challenging—is possible.

For those who have walked the path of anxiety, depression, trauma, or grief, therapy is the hand that helps them keep walking when they feel like they can't go any further. It is the reminder that no matter how overwhelming life may feel, there is a way through. In this sense, therapy isn't just helpful; it's lifesaving. It's not a privilege for the few, but a crucial resource for anyone trying to find solid ground in an often tumultuous world.

Chapter 10 Quiet Strength

In her darkest night,

Voices of love pull her through,

Strength in every hand.

(Maya sits across from her therapist, Dr. Patel, in a small, warmly lit office. A soft hum of instrumental music plays faintly in the background. Maya's fingers fidget with the hem of her sweater as she exhales heavily.)

Dr. Patel: *You seem deep in thought, Maya. What's on your mind?*

Maya: *(shrugs) I don't know… nothing, I guess. It just feels like no matter how hard I try, I keep ending up at the same dead end.*

Dr. Patel: *The job search?*

Maya: *(nods) It's all I do, all day, every day. I apply, I wait, I hope… and then its not the perfect place I wanted. Over and over again. I don't know why I keep putting myself through it.*

Dr. Patel: *That sounds exhausting.*

Maya: *It is. But what choice do I have? I just want my life back—the version of it where I felt useful, independent… normal.*

Dr. Patel: *And right now, you don't feel any of those things?*

Maya: *(shaking her head) No. Right now, I feel stuck. Trapped. I'm glued to my phone, chasing opportunities* *that never work out. And when I do get an offer, it's for a job that's too far, or something I can't realistically take. It's like the universe is playing some cruel joke on me.*

Dr. Patel: *I hear a lot of frustration in your voice.*

Maya: *Of course, I'm frustrated! I've done everything I'm supposed to do. I worked hard, I pushed through all of the hospital stays, all of the setbacks—wasn't that enough? Shouldn't I be allowed to move forward now?*

Dr. Patel: *I can see how much this means to you. And how painful it is to feel like the world isn't responding in the way you need it to.*

Maya: *(softly) It's not just painful. It's terrifying. What if this is it? What if I never get back to where I was?*

Dr. Patel: *That's a big fear. One that makes a lot of sense, given everything you've been through. But tell me, what does "getting back to where you were" really mean to you?*

Maya: *I don't know… being busy again, having a purpose, not feeling like a burden to my family.*

Dr. Patel: *Do you believe that your worth is tied to your productivity?*

Maya: I don't know. Maybe? I mean, it's not like I'm doing anything meaningful right now.

Dr. Patel: You're healing. That's meaningful.

Maya: (smirks slightly) That sounds like something people say when there's nothing else to say.

Dr. Patel: It's something I say because I believe it. You've gone through a massive upheaval in your life, Maya. And instead of giving up, you're still here. You're still trying. That matters.

Maya: Trying doesn't pay the bills.

Dr. Patel: No, it doesn't. And I know you need stability.

What if, instead of seeing them as roadblocks, you saw them as detours?

Maya: Detours to where?

Dr. Patel: That's something we can figure out together. But maybe—just maybe—where you're meant to be isn't exactly where you planned.

Maya: (quietly) My mom said something similar. That maybe God has a bigger plan for me.

Dr. Patel: And how did that sit with you?

__Maya:__ I wanted to believe her. I really did. But it's hard to have faith in something I can't see.

__Dr. Patel:__ That's understandable. But faith—whether in God, in yourself, or in the process—doesn't require having all the answers right now. It just requires you to keep moving, even when you're unsure of the destination.

__Maya:__ (softly) What if I get lost?

__Dr. Patel:__ Then we'll find another way. You're not doing this alone, Maya.

Her therapist then taught her about the **ABC Model.**

The "ABC" model, often used in cognitive behavioural therapy (CBT), is a framework for understanding how our beliefs about events shape our emotional and behavioural responses.

A - Act (or Activating Event)

This is the objective event or situation that triggers the emotional response. It's a neutral fact, something that happens, without any emotional weight attached. In this case, the "Act" or activating event is the fact that she doesn't currently have a job. This is an objective reality, just a fact.

B - Belief

This is how the person interprets the Act. It's the lens through which they see the situation, which often influences their emotions. In this example, the belief is that because she doesn't have a job, she is "worthless." This belief is subjective and reflects her perception of herself in the situation. It's important to recognize that the belief isn't necessarily true or based in reality, but it has a significant impact on how she feels.

C - Consequence

This is the emotional or behavioural outcome that follows from the belief. In this case, the consequence is that she feels sad because of the belief that she is worthless without a job. The emotional consequence is a direct result of the belief, not the fact that she doesn't have a job.

The power of the ABC model lies in understanding that it's not the event itself (A) that causes the emotional consequence (C), but rather the belief (B) about the event. By changing her belief (e.g., "Not having a job right now doesn't mean I'm worthless"), she could change the emotional consequence (feeling sad) into something more positive or neutral.

This framework encourages people to question and challenge their beliefs to create healthier emotional responses to life's events.

Alongside her therapist, there was another person who played a pivotal role in her recovery: her close friend, who also happened to be a psychologist.

Maya's friend had been a constant presence throughout her life, someone who had seen her at her best and at her worst. Unlike many of Maya's other friends, this one understood the complexities of mental health on a deeper level. Having both the professional insight and the personal bond, her friend offered Maya something rare—a blend of empathy, compassion, and clinical understanding. Though their conversations never felt like formal therapy sessions, her friend provided her with an additional layer of support, helping Maya process her emotions in ways that complemented her work with her therapist.

Maya: (*staring out the window*) "I don't know Ananya, but I don't understand. It feels like I'm just going in, talking about the same stuff, and nothing changes. Am I just wasting my time?"

Ananya: (*gently nudges Maya's shoulder*) "You're not wasting your time. The thing about therapy is that it's not about immediate fixes. It's about untangling all those emotions and thoughts that you've been carrying around. It's about giving yourself the space to understand why you feel the way you do, and that takes time. Think of it like planting a tree. You won't see the roots or the growth at first, but something is happening beneath the surface."

Maya: (*pauses, considering this*) "So, you're saying... I'm still making progress, even if I don't see it?"

Ananya: (*nodding*) "Exactly. Every time you go in and talk about your feelings, every time you dig a little deeper or confront something difficult, that's progress. You're doing the work, even if it doesn't feel like it right away. It's like building a muscle. You can't always see the results immediately, but with every session, you're getting stronger—mentally and emotionally."

Maya: (*frowning slightly*) "But... doesn't therapy mean something's wrong with me? Doesn't it mean I'm mentally weak or broken?"

Ananya: (*shakes her head gently*) "Maya, that's a huge misconception. Therapy is not for the weak. Therapy is for the brave. It's for people who are strong enough to admit that they need help, who are willing to face their pain and work through it. It's not a sign of weakness; it's a sign of strength. It takes courage to confront your fears, to go deep into your mind and understand your emotions. Most people avoid that, but you're doing it. You're taking control of your mental health, and that's incredibly powerful."

Maya: (*looks down for a moment, taking it all in*) "I never really thought about it like that. I guess... I'm afraid people will think I'm weak for going to therapy and cry."

Ananya: (*softly*) "I know that fear. But the truth is, you're doing something that most people aren't brave enough to do. You're prioritizing your well-being, and you're actively working on healing. You're strong, Maya. You are *so* much stronger than you give yourself credit for."

Maya: (*nodding*) "I'll try to keep that in mind. Maybe I'm not as stuck as I think."

Ananya: (*smiling warmly*) "Exactly. You're making progress every single day."

Together, her therapist and Ananya became her pillars of strength. Maya's therapist guided her through the intricate process of self-reflection, helping her untangle the web of emotions that had trapped her for so long.Meanwhile, her friend provided a more informal, yet deeply valuable, layer of support. In moments when therapy felt heavy, Maya's friend would remind her of the progress she had made, helping her see beyond the immediate struggles.

At the same time, Maya's sister and brother-in-law played an equally crucial role during this period. They offered her unwavering support, not only in words but through action. Recognizing the toll that her mental health challenges had taken, her family became an essential part of her healing process, encouraging her to stay engaged in various activities and conversations.

They kept her mind occupied during the difficult days, gently drawing her into shared moments that helped her navigate through the darker periods. Whether it was family meals, car drives, or simply watching a movie together, these small yet significant gestures reminded Maya that she wasn't alone in her journey.

"See that thoughts and feelings are like train that enters a station and then leaves; be like the station, not like a passenger."

Rupert spira, from The Ashes of Love

At the same time, one of her friends visited her every day, providing invaluable support.It wasn't just the consistency of their visits but the unspoken understanding between them that brought comfort. The presence alone helped her manage her anxieties and dispel the depressive thoughts that had been weighing on her. Maya didn't talk much and had been quiet for a long time, often feeling blank with her thoughts. Each day, her friend would bring a laptop and work quietly beside her. She didn't need to say much; simply having someone nearby brought her comfort and made her feel alive and happy. The sheer act of showing up day after day gave Maya a sense of stability she desperately needed.

Aditya: (setting his laptop down beside her, glancing at Maya with a soft smile) "You feeling okay today?"

Maya doesn't answer, but she gives him a small nod and a faint smile, her eyes tired but appreciative.

Aditya: (pulling out his work notebook, starting to type but looking at her occasionally) "You know, I'm not going anywhere. I'll be right here, just like always."

Aditya: (after a pause, speaking gently) "You don't have to say anything, Maya. I get it. I'm not here to make you talk if you don't feel like it. But I want you to know, I'm here, and I'm not leaving. You don't have to be alone in this."

(Maya's eyes soften, and she gives a small but sincere smile)

Aditya: *(glances at her and his voice steady) "Some days are harder than others, I know. But remember, one day at a time. And you're not going through this by yourself. I'm right here with you, every step of the way."*

Aditya: *"I'm proud of you, Maya. Even on the tough days. You're stronger than you think."*

Maya: *(after a long pause, she looks at him, her voice barely above a whisper) "Thank you... for everything."*

There were no more words exchanged, but in that silence, Maya felt something shift within her. It wasn't just the absence of conversation, but the presence of someone who truly understood her without needing to fill the space with endless words. The quiet companionship, the steady assurance of Aditya's support, made her feel less alone. It was in this unspoken bond that she found a kind of comfort—subtle, yet profound. And for the first time in a long while, she felt okay just sitting in that stillness with him, knowing she didn't need to speak to be seen.

During those challenging times, it became clear to her that she wanted to overcome the difficulties she was facing. Her friend's daily visits played a crucial role in helping her come out of that dark place. He not only supported her but also showed immense patience throughout her recovery. Aditya's unwavering commitment reminded her that even in her most vulnerable moments, she didn't have to carry the burden of her struggles alone. These small acts of love—from long walks around the neighborhood to cups of tea shared in quiet understanding—were profound reminders that healing didn't happen in isolation. Aditya's patience and unwavering support, along with the support of her family, gave her the strength and reassurance that she would soon emerge from this turmoil. Their collective encouragement was a beacon of hope, confirming that brighter days were ahead.

"Surround yourself with only people who are going to lift you higher."

Oprah Winfrey

Chapter 11 The Journey Within

Light breaks through the clouds,

Peace blooms where darkness once dwelled,

Her soul shines again.

Her thoughts turned to the people who mattered most to her.They were a constant presence in her mind, the individuals who inspired her to push through the toughest of challenges. Visualizing their faces, their unwavering support, and the trust they had in her gave Maya the mental anchor she so desperately needed in that moment. Their presence, even in her thoughts, was enough to keep her grounded.

"I can't let them down," she reminded herself. *"They believe in me, and I need to believe in myself too."* This inner dialogue became her mantra, a way to focus on something beyond the discomfort, something larger than herself. Their influence was so profound that it helped her stay calm, even in a situation that would have otherwise felt overwhelming.

Despite the hardships, Maya knew she had to keep fighting—not just for herself, but for those who believed in her. It wasn't just about surviving the illness anymore; it was about reclaiming her strength and her identity, no matter how many setbacks came her way.

Maya looked at her reflection and thought, *"I'm not the only one going through this. There are others my age who are facing even harder battles and yet show the strength to keep going. They're not shattered; they're resilient. If they can rise and face each day with courage, then I can find that strength in myself too."*

Despite her struggle, the remarkable aspect was her acute awareness of her own emotions. She recognized her sadness and acknowledged the depression she was going through. She understood that the heaviness she felt was not an intrinsic part of who she was, but rather a temporary state she would eventually overcome. This self-awareness became her anchor, as she continually reminded herself that these emotions were fleeting and would pass in time.

"The first thing you need to do is get in touch of negative feelings that you're not aware of. Get in touch with those feelings first."

Anthony de mello, Awareness: conversations with the masters

"There is depression there right now, there are hurt feelings there right now, but let it be, leave it alone. It will pass. Everything passes, everything."

Anthony de mello, Awakening conversations with the masters.

Amidst the overwhelming darkness of her depression, a spark of determination began to flicker within her. Maya realized that, despite the deep pain and despair she had endured, she had a vision for her life -a vision of living not just a normal life, but a life of purpose and significance. She wanted to live a larger life, one that would not only bring her fulfillment but also inspire others to seek out the best in themselves. She envisioned a life that could motivate others to rise above their challenges and strive for greatness.

With this newfound resolve, Maya made the decision to take control of her life, to actively work on healing herself from the inside out. She knew it wouldn't be easy and that the road ahead would be filled with obstacles, but she was determined to push through.

She started to make small changes in her daily routine, focusing on self-care and personal growth. She sought out new experiences and challenges that would help her grow, both mentally and emotionally. She reached out for support when she needed it, understanding that she didn't have to face this journey alone. Slowly but surely, she began to see progress in herself-her mind becoming clearer, her heart a little lighter, and her spirit more resilient.

As she continued to work on herself, she found that her life began to take on new meaning. She was no longer merely surviving; she was living with intention and purpose. Each day became an opportunity to move closer to the life she envisioned-a life that was larger than her pain, larger than her fears, and larger than the limitations her illness had once imposed on her.

In time, her transformation became evident not just to herself, but to those around her. Her journey from the depths of despair to a life of purpose became a beacon of hope for others. Her story inspired those who were struggling, showing them that even after the darkest night, the sun will shine. She had set out to live a larger life, and in doing so, she not only changed her own destiny but also touched the lives of others, motivating them to seek out the larger, more fulfilling lives they deserved.

Her therapist observed with a mix of surprise and admiration the rapid pace of her recovery, commenting that they had rarely seen anyone make such significant progress in such a short period of time. The steady improvement in her emotional state, her renewed sense of purpose, and her ability to regain control over her thoughts stood out as exceptional.

When the therapist shared these thoughts during one of their sessions, she smiled softly and replied, *"It's all because of the support of my people"* She went on to explain how their constant encouragement and presence had been her greatest strength. They had stood by her every step of the way, offering not only reassurance but also reminding her of the spiritual values and resilience she had cultivated since childhood. It was their unwavering belief in her ability to overcome this phase that empowered her to fight back against the darkness and reclaim her life.

The transformation was not just physical, but emotional and mental as well. Where others might have grown weary, she became stronger. Where some might have lost hope, she gained wisdom. Her ability to endure and learn from adversity became one of her greatest strengths.

She emerged from the ordeal not as a victim of circumstance, but as a young woman who had transformed herself through grit and determination. What began as a series of medical challenges had shaped her into someone with a deep well of resilience. She had learned how to navigate life's uncertainties with grace, and her capacity to overcome adversity became a defining characteristic of her life.

Opportunities in disguise: What we often label as negative experiences are, in fact, opportunities in disguise. Difficult situations push us out of our comfort zones, forcing us to adapt, rethink our strategies, and develop new skills. These experiences can be catalysts for significant personal growth.

By changing our perspective on negative experiences, we can approach them with a mindset that seeks out the lessons and growth opportunities they offer.

Pain, whether emotional or physical, is often a powerful teacher. It demands our attention and forces us to confront aspects of ourselves or our lives that we might otherwise ignore. Pain can reveal our vulnerabilities, prompting us to strengthen them, or it can highlight areas in need of change, encouraging us to take action.

Experiencing pain often leads to a deeper understanding of ourselves and others. It can foster empathy, resilience, and a greater appreciation for life's complexities. Those who have faced and transcended pain often emerge with greater wisdom and a stronger sense of purpose.

To transcend pain, one must first experience it fully. This means acknowledging and feeling the pain rather than avoiding or suppressing it. By going through the pain, we learn to cope with it, understand its causes, and ultimately, overcome it.

This resilience and clarity of mind did not come by chance. It was a result of her upbringing and the environment in which she was raised. From a young age, her parents introduced her to the world of spirituality through their own practices and conversations. Spirituality was woven into the fabric of their household, and discussions on mindfulness, the nature of the self, and the importance of inner peace were a regular part of their daily life. Her parents often engaged her in dialogues about the teachings of great philosophers and spiritual leaders, encouraging her to read and reflect on profound ideas that shaped her understanding of the world.

As she grew older, she developed a love for reading and delved into books that expanded on the teachings she first learned at home. The books, along with her parents' early influence, provided her with a solid foundation to face life's challenges.

When depression threatened to overwhelm her, it was this grounding that helped her navigate through the pain. The teachings she had absorbed became more than just theoretical—they transformed into guiding principles that allowed her to detach from the negativity and maintain hope. She learned to view her sadness as a temporary state, something she could observe rather than become consumed by.

It was this combined wisdom from her parents and the literature she explored that ultimately guided her through the darkest moments, enabling her not only to survive but to emerge stronger, with a profound sense of resilience and inner strength.

"When the going gets tough, the tough truly gets going" seemed to echo from every sentence, giving her courage to face the day. The motivational words she absorbed acted like fuel to her fire, pushing her to keep her chin up and keep moving forward when life seemed an uphill battle.

However, her greatest inspiration came from her father, a man who had fought his battles with the strength of a lion. He taught her that it's not about waiting for the storm to pass, but about learning to dance in the rain. His courage and tenacity stood like a towering lighthouse amidst the tempest, guiding her to never give up, to weather the storm, and to find a silver lining in even the darkest clouds.

Seeing him face adversity head-on, she realized that *"every cloud has a silver lining"* and that *"falling down is part of life, but getting back up is living."* His presence was the rock she leaned on, and his words, like those of her beloved books, were the anchor that kept her steady when the waves of illness tried to pull her under.

With the wisdom of her books and the example of her father, she transformed her suffering into a source of strength, embodying the belief that *"what doesn't kill you only makes you stronger."*

"She stood in the storm, and when the wind did not blow her way, she adjusted her sails."

Elizabeth Edwards

"I learned that courage was not the absence of fear, but the triumph over it. The brave man is not he who does not feel afraid, but he who conquers that fear."

Nelson Mandela

Emotional resilience : Emotional resilience, the ability to bounce back from setbacks, is a key trait of successful individuals. By maintaining control over their emotions and responses, they navigate life's challenges without being overwhelmed by them. This resilience is rooted in a well-managed inner world.

When you control your thoughts and responses, you start living intentionally. You make choices that align with your goals and values, rather than being swayed by external pressures or fleeting emotions. This intentionality is what steers towards your desired destiny.

By recognising that you have control over your inner world, you empower yourself to create the life you want.

Maya came to a profound realization that all along, the divine presence she had been tirelessly searching for in various sacred places-the four pilgrimage sites, temples, and idols -was actually residing within her. The true essence of the divine, the sanctity of the temple, and the presence of the deity were not external entities that she needed to find outside of herself. Instead, they existed within her own being, inherently part of who she was.

This realization itself was transformative for her. It shifted her perspective from one of outward searching to one of inward discovery. Maya understood that all the answers she had been looking for externally- about life, existence, and her purpose-could be found within herself, through the recognition of the divine that had always been a part of her. This inner journey of self-discovery and spiritual awakening promised to bring her the peace and understanding she had long desired.

136

For many years, she had not acknowledged this inner divinity, but now she understood that it was crucial to do so. Recognizing the divine within herself was not just an abstract spiritual idea; it was the key to unlocking the answers to all the deep, existential questions she had been grappling with for so long. She realized that by turning inward and embracing this inner divine presence, she would find the clarity and wisdom she had been seeking.

This understanding brought her to the awareness that her search for God in the external world was unnecessary because the divine had always been with her, dwelling inside her. The reason she hadn't felt this presence before was simply because she hadn't recognized it. Her quest for spiritual fulfilment had been directed outwardly, but the true journey she needed to embark on was inward-to recognize and - connect with the divine within herself.

The last stage of kubler-ross theory:- **ACCEPTANCE**

She also came to the realisation that instead of asking "why me"? One must focus on the other good things they have in life.Often, when we encounter hardships, our immediate reaction is to ask, "Why me?"—as if we are being unfairly singled out by life or by a higher power. However, this way of thinking focuses on the negative and can make the challenge feel even more overwhelming. By questioning why something bad is happening, we add an emotional burden to an already difficult situation.

Instead, the suggestion is to practice gratitude, even in the face of adversity. It's natural to feel sad and overwhelmed, and it's understandable that shifting focus to the brighter side can seem difficult at times. However, consciously choosing to reflect on the things that are still going well—no matter how small—can make a world of difference. After all, **mindset is everything**; the more you nurture a grateful outlook, the more resilience you build to navigate challenges can transform even the toughest moments into opportunities for growth.

Two people can face identical situations, yet come away with vastly different interpretations simply because of the mindsets they carry. One sees opportunity in adversity, viewing setbacks as stepping stones toward growth, while the other sees only roadblocks and reasons to give up. The situations themselves haven't changed; it's the lens through which they are viewed that makes all the difference. Thus, nurturing a positive mindset isn't about ignoring the difficulties or pretending that everything is always fine. Rather, it's about training the mind to look for the lessons, to spot the glimmers of hope that might

otherwise go unnoticed, and to build resilience in the
process.

*"Everything can be taken from a man but one thing: the
last of the human freedoms—to choose one's attitude in
any given set of circumstances, to choose one's own
way."*

Viktor E. Frankl, Man's search for Meaning

*"You may not control all the events that happen to you,
but you can decide not to be reduced by them."*

Maya Angelou

*"The greatest discovery of all time is that a person can
change his future by merely changing his attitude."*

Oprah Winfrey

Embracing these philosophies means recognizing that
while we often have little control over what happens to
us, we always have control over how we respond. It's
the belief that, despite external circumstances, there is
power in choosing how we interpret and react to life's
events. With a growth mindset, failure is not the end but

a valuable learning experience; criticism becomes a
tool for self-improvement, not a wound to the ego.

EPILOGUE

"And once the storm is over, you won't remember how you made it through, how you managed to survive. You won't even be sure, in fact, whether the storm is really over. But one thing is certain. When you come out of the storm, you won't be the same person who walked in. That's what this storm's all about."
— Haruki Murakami

Maya had reached a point in her journey where she no longer saw her disease as an insurmountable obstacle, but rather as a part of her life that she could manage and live with. She had learned that she was not defined by her disease, nor did her struggles or challenges determine who she was. Her identity went beyond the illness she had battled or the difficulties she had faced.

"These are just parts of my life, not the essence of who I am as a person," she would remind herself. *"I have strengths, passions, and qualities that make me unique, and they are far more significant than the health issues or setbacks I might encounter. My disease and problems are just circumstances, not my identity."*

She had learned how to navigate her daily routines with a newfound sense of awareness and acceptance. Instead of feeling overwhelmed by the unpredictability of her illness, she had developed coping mechanisms that allowed her to maintain a sense of control over her life. She understood the limitations her condition imposed, but rather than letting them define her, she adapted, shaping a life that worked for her rather than against her.

And in doing so, she built something remarkable.

Maya had taken the leap and started her own business—something she had once only dreamed of. What had once seemed impossible now flourished into a reality. She poured her heart, soul, and 500% of her energy into it, creating something that was entirely hers.

"Life is not about waiting for the storm to pass but about learning to dance in the rain."
—Vivian Greene

Through a combination of medical treatment, faith, and personal resilience, Maya had found a balance between managing her health and living a fulfilling life. She had become attuned to her body's signals, knowing when to rest and when to push forward. With time, she gained confidence in her ability to handle flare-ups, setbacks, and the emotional toll of her condition.

Rather than allowing her illness to dominate her thoughts, she had integrated it into her life without letting it overshadow her goals, relationships, or happiness. Maya was no longer simply surviving. She acknowledged her pain, but she was now thriving. She had transformed from a patient bound by fear and uncertainty into a woman with purpose, fully aware of how to coexist with her challenges while still chasing her dreams.

"Although the world is full of suffering, it is also full of overcoming of it."
—Helen Keller

And now, as she lay on her bed, surrounded by the quiet hum of the night, she felt a profound sense of transformation. She had emerged stronger, no longer defined by her illness but by her resilience and unwavering hope.

Maya, a lifelong Bollywood fan, had always found comfort in the words of her favorite film, "*Anand*", a movie she had watched countless times since childhood. As the weight of the night settled around her, she whispered the iconic lines from the film to herself :

Maya (whispering, almost as if she were speaking to the universe): *"Zindagi aur maut toh upar wale ke haath me hai jahapana, usse na toh aap badal sakte ho, na mein... hum sab toh rangmanch ki kathputliyan hain, jinki dor upar wale ki ungliyon mein bandhi hai. Kab, kaun, kaise uthega, ye koi nahi bata sakta hai."*

__Her Reflection (in the quiet of the room, a voice from within):__ *"But what you can control... is how you live. How you fight. How you carry yourself in this journey, regardless of what comes."*

__Maya (a soft, knowing smile tugging at her lips):__ *"Maybe that's the only thing that matters. That I'm still here. Still fighting."*

__Her Reflection (gently):__ *"Yes, Maya. That's enough."*

The journey ahead was uncertain. The road had never truly been truly smooth. But she had learned something important along the way—there was strength in simply showing up, in facing whatever came next, even if she didn't have all the answers.

And that, somehow, was enough.

That was the beauty of it.

With a small but satisfactory smile, she turned off the lights, closed her eyes, stepping forward into whatever came next.

As the final words of Maya's story lingered in the air, something about the tone shifted, taking on a deeper, more intimate feel. *"It wasn't just Maya's journey, you know. It's something deeper, something that many of us go through. The paths we walk, the battles we face, they leave their mark. And, in the end, we're never the same as when we began."*

"It's not just a line I wrote; it's a truth I've come to know all too well. Pain and struggle have a way of transforming you, whether you're ready for it or not. You don't just survive through it—you come out of it different, stronger, changed. That's the beauty of it all."

And suddenly, everything clicked—the lessons, the growth, the quiet acceptance. The story, though it was Maya's, felt like it had been told through the eyes of someone who had known that journey intimately. The battles, the scars, the transformation—it was clear now that Maya's story had been something far more personal, something that transcended the pages.

"When you've suffered long enough... you don't just survive. You change."

— Mahek Trivedi